I0592738

NEVER GO HOME

A STORY OF WORLD WAR II'S AFFECT ON A FAMILY

MATT PELLER

Never Go Home is a work of historical fiction. Apart from the well-known actual people, events and locales that figure in the narrative, all names, characters, places and incidents are the products of the author's imagination and are used fictionally. Any resemblance to current events or locales, or to living persons is entirely coincidental.

Never Go Home: A Story of World War II's Affect on a Family
Copyright © 2018 Matthew Thomas Peller. All rights reserved. No part of this book may be reproduced or retransmitted in any form or by any means without the written permission of the publisher.

Published by Love My 4 Es Publishing
Sonora, California

ISBN: 978-0-692-14700-9 (paperback)
ISBN: 978-0-692-14702-3 (ebook)
LCCN: 2018907543

Registration Number TXu 2-085-746
Effective Date of registration: February 08, 2018

THIS BOOK IS DEDICATED TO:

My wife Carmella,
who has seen me disappear into my office,
for over a year now, and has not complained.

To my editors, Jill and Larry.

To the rest of the Sonora Writers' Group,
who have critiqued my writing these past few years.

And to Alyse Homan Walker,
the talented young artist who created my book cover.

TABLE OF CONTENTS

INTRODUCTION

Banat was once part of the Habsburg Kingdom of Hungary. Looking at its history, will give a better understanding of the Swabian people, who comprise this book's principal characters.

Habsburg Austria drove the Ottoman Turks out of Banat in 1718. The Habsburg emperors then colonized it with Germans. They were happy to come, due to the unsettled and violent situation in their homeland. Settling mainly along the Danube River, they came to be known as Danube Swabians.

But Hungarians were in the majority in Banat. And Serbians were a close third, right behind the Swabians in population. There was also a minority Jewish population, centered in the cities and larger towns. And there were other ethnic groups including Slovaks, Russians and Croatians.

The Butscher family immigrated to Banat in 1742 and chose to live along the Danube River in Apatin. The Diplichs were next in 1743 and settled north, also along the river in Batina. The Gensers came about twenty years later to Tiimisoara in the east. And the Eiberts in 1796 to the center of Apatin.

Konrad's grandfather, Stefan Butscher, finished construction of their house during 1888 and the inn during 1889. All of his children were born in that house, including Mathias in 1890.

Leading up to the First World War there was much ethnic tension and bloodshed. The Kingdom of Serbia occupied the southern part of Banat for a time. And there was an unsuccessful Hungarian revolt against Austria, which resulted in a dual monarchy. But the desire for an independent Hungary never faded.

The assassination of Archduke Franz Ferdinand of Austria, heir presumptive to the Austro-Hungarian throne, and his wife Sophie, occurred on 28 June 1914. The political objective of the assassination by the Black Hand was to break off Austria-Hungary's southern provinces, with their Serbian majorities, so they could be combined into a Yugoslavia.

The assassination led directly to the First World War. Austria-Hungary declared war, and that triggered responses leading to war between most European states. Austria-Hungary was tied up in heavy fighting against Serbia and Italy for the rest of the war and did not supply the anticipated troop-levels to fight Russia.

The Trianon Treaty of 1920 punished Austria by giving independence to Hungary and dividing the Banat into southern Hungary (Bacs-Bodrog), northeastern Serbia (Vojvodina) and western Romania (Timis). This treaty's terms were very unpopular in Vojvodina which was still fifty percent Hungarian and Swabian. Both being Catholic they were natural allies.

Mathias met Eva Theresia Eibert at a social held by the Church of the Heart of Jesus, outside of Apatin. They married and their children were baptized there, Theresia in 1909, Konrad in 1915 and Stefan in 1921. Grandfather Stefan died of the flu in October, 1917. When he died, Mathias was his only surviving son, the others having died in the war.

Miklos Horthy was Vice-Admiral and Commander of the Fleet in the Austro-Hungarian Navy. He had seen action in the Otranto Raid and the Battle of the Strait of Otranto. In 1919, following a series of revolutions and external interventions in Hungary, he returned to Budapest with the National Army.

Horthy was subsequently invited, in fact begged, to become Regent of the Kingdom by parliament. He led a conservative government through the interwar period. Horthy banned both the Hungarian Communist Party, and the fascist Arrow Cross Party. He pursued a foreign policy that's main goal was to regain territories lost under the Treaty of Trianon.

Sophia Eibert met Michael Genser when she was sixteen. It was August and his regiment formed-up in Apatin. They were waiting for their marching orders, to head south for what would be the Battle of Cer in Serbia. She was a beautiful teenager and caught his eye, as he sat in the shade of a tree, and she strolled by, flirting with the soldiers. He had to get her name.

The next time she saw him was at a field hospital. She had volunteered as an aide. He had been wounded in the Austrian defeat and was laying on a cot with his head bandaged. He recovered, married Sophie, went back into combat, survived the war and settled down with her in Apatin. Their twin sons, Ludwig and Filipp, were born in 1920.

It was June, 1941 and Hungary needed experienced soldiers. He volunteered and went off to war again, this time at age forty-four. She took a job at her sister's business, as a waitress in the tavern.

1

KONRAD

"I do." The words she wanted to hear from me.

"And do you, Magdalena Roth, take Konrad Butscher to be your lawfully wedded husband?" She stumbled over her answer, but caught herself, and gave the right one.

And then, "I now pronounce you man and wife".

And I thought to myself, *"I have my new wife, my farm, my family, my country, my church and my God. I'm truly a blessed and happy man. How beautiful is this special day!"*

But as we walked out and down the steps of Sacred Heart Catholic Church, we saw the two fighter planes that roared low overhead. I remember vividly the swastikas on their rear fuselages and the feeling that the timing was an omen. I said, "War is on our doorstep."

Later when the celebrations were over and we were alone, Maggie asked me, "Konrad, what will you do if Hungary goes to war?"

I said something like, "Let's worry about that some other time."

But she wanted to talk about it then. She said, "Those fighter planes are in my head. They're breaking the mood of such a lovely day."

I tried to be understanding, and gave some thought about what to say.

"You've heard me talk about the folly of this expansionism by the Germans. They will drag everyone into war sooner or later. I will try to avoid going, but if I'm drafted, I'll do my duty."

That seemed to make her feel better.

She said, "It will be my job then to convince you to stay home. You love me that much. I know that you do. And don't worry, there will be plenty of volunteers to fight. I'm sure of that."

Our home was a small farm house with stamped mud and straw walls outside of Futog—a village of Danube Swabians. Maggie and I met there, at a church dance.

In just a few weeks the magic started for both of us.

We Swabians were long established German emigrants, fully Hungarianised. I would often hear Maggie's father declare, "We Swabians are more loyal to Hungary than even the Hungarians."

I was twenty-six. There were few men near my age due to the last generation's casualties in the Great War. And many of those men were farmers. Our farm had three cows, two pigs and two horses. One horse was for plowing and the other for riding. Corn and potatoes were our main crops.

Maggie was right, the neighboring large commercial center of Novi Sad was very pro-German. Eleven weeks ago, German and Hungarian troops had attacked Serbia. They had quickly retaken Vojvodina from the Serbs, making the whole district of Bacs-Bodrog part of Hungary again.

That's when Maggie said, "This is finally a good time to set the date for our wedding. Now that the fighting has moved away from here."

It was our first morning as man and wife and we were at home. She got up first and made a breakfast of sausage, eggs and biscuits.

I stretched and said, "What a great morning! I'll go to town later for some supplies that I need. Do you need anything?"

It was June 22nd, 1941. I went, and came back to her with the news. "As I predicted, Germany has invaded Russia!" By August they had taken Smolensk; by September they were at Leningrad's door; and by December threatening Moscow and barely pushed back from it.

In a few days, my younger brother, Stefan, came to dinner.

When Maggie heard she started a *hasenpfeffer*, marinated rabbit, for him. A treat which took several days to prepare properly. Her mother had taught her how. Stefan was a favorite of hers. She told me more than once that she had always wanted a brother near her age, which was twenty-one. Stefan was twenty.

Over coffee and a strudel, Stefan told us, "I am going to join the Einstazgruppen and fight right here and not in some place far away like Russia. The Russians haven't done anything. It's the Serbs who have never stopped fighting us. Now it's guerilla warfare. First the Chetniks, ex-Yugoslav Army, and now the Partisans, Communists. I'm going to take the SS up on their recruiting offer. I'll be an officer in the paramilitary police before you know it."

I was not in favor and told Stefan, "That's very patriotic of you, but I've heard bad things about those people. They use very brutal tactics. The regular army needs help. If you must fight, why don't you just sign up with them? It would be a better choice, more noble." But it was no use. He was always thickheaded.

Stefan continued, "We had every right to overturn that damned Trianon Treaty. It's been long enough since the Great War. We should have our territory and our people back. All Hungarians whether they're Magyar, Székely, Swabian, Slovak, Ruthenian or Jew should be part of Hungary. It's the Serbs who are killing us! And I don't trust the damned Romanians either."

On a hot day in early July, Stefan left for training.

Chetnik raids were occurring and recruits were needed immediately. He stopped to say goodbye as he started on his two-kilometer walk to Futog. A truck would pick him up there.

I grasped his shoulder as we shook hands. "Be strong." was all that I allowed myself to say. There was no point in having him go off to war with us arguing.

Maggie wept as she said, "We love you. And I'm afraid for you. And for us, that we might never see you again. Come home to us safe. I'll pray."

Shortly after that Stefan wrote, "The Germans are forming a new division from German speaking Danube Swabian volunteers. The Police Leader has encouraged us recent police recruits to make the switch. I've been commissioned as a Lieutenant and I'm enclosing a picture of me in my new uniform." He did look handsome in his long leather overcoat and M1937 pistol as his sidearm.

In August I read in the newspaper that the new division, the 7th SS Division, was under-manned. The SS court in Belgrade was imposing mandatory military obligations on all Swabians in Bacs-Bodrog in order to fill the ranks.

"Maggie, this is bad. It's the first time that I've heard of non-Reich Germans being drafted. I guess I knew that it could happen, but never thought that it would. It changes everything. I have to do something. But I don't know what."

Maggie said, "We must go somewhere that they won't find us. I'm not going to let you be dragged off to war!" And she meant it. We began discussing alternatives.

My parents, Mathias and Eva Butscher, lived north of Novi Sad in the town of Apatin. It is on the border with Croatia. They owned a small inn, tavern and the bakery next door.

My older sister, Theresia, her husband, Johann Diplich, and their sons Mathias and Adam also lived there. Mathias was fifteen and Adam was fourteen. Johann was the baker and loved his profession. Theresia took care of their two sons and handled the bakery's paperwork.

My mother's younger sister, my aunt, Sophia Genser lived there as well. As did her twin sons, Ludwig and Filipp. They were twenty-one years old, which was perfect for the military. Michael Genser, her husband, their father, was already in the Army. He was fighting in the Ukraine since June. Sophia and the boys worked in the tavern.

Aunt Sophia and her sons, heard of Michael's death, at Izium on October 14th. Ludwig and Filipp volunteered immediately. We learned they were assigned to the newly formed 2nd Army for training. They were in its III Corp, Light Division 6. The rumor was that it was under-manned and didn't have anti-tank weapons. I thought, "Oh great! But that can't be the way they'll be deployed. Nobody can be that stupid."

Maggie and I decided to move in with my parents. It was a good idea, except for my feeling the loss of independence. "Here I go back to my parents' house. It was just five years since I moved to Futog, and purchased my farm. It was far away from my parents. My independence was that important to me."

I sold off the cows and the pigs. The market was good. We loaded our best possessions onto our two-wheeled cart. I hitched up the plow-horse, and put Maggie on the riding horse. We made the eighty-kilometer journey and they welcomed us warmly. After selling the horses and cart, I stayed out of public sight for months. I hid until the new division deployed.

Anna, Maggie's older sister, heard of our move and visited us there. Her husband, Christian Theer, was in the army, fighting in the Ukraine. She had gotten only an occasional letter. In them she learned that they had crossed the Dnieper River.

"I guess that means they're having some success, but I'm so worried. Will you pray with me, for him?" she asked.

"Yes, of course. Let's kneel." So, we prayed for him and for the army.

Maggie shared with me later, "I never think of Christian as a brother. I prayed for my father instead. My father lives there with Anna and Christian and won't move out. He doesn't want to leave Anna alone with him. That Christian is a real bastard when he's drunk, which I understand is always. Even my father is afraid of him."

Christian was in the Mobile Corp of the 44,000-strong Carpathian Group. The newspaper said, *"These brave warriors advanced across the Dnieper River on October 12th and helped destroy Soviet units near Izium. Then on the 21st, they crossed the River Donets and advanced, in heavy action. Finally, they were withdrawn from the front-line on November 10th. And now they've returned to Hungary, having marched 1,770 kilometers, and suffered 2,992 casualties."*

Christian was given a medal and a one-month furlough. He returned home on November 20th.

Maggie went to visit them a few days later. Just before she knocked on the door she heard him yelling, "Get me another Weifert! And don't say anything. If I drink myself to death, it will at least stop this damn headache. Another beer! If I have to get it myself, you'll regret it."

When Maggie returned home, she said, "I couldn't believe my ears. When I went in, he realized that I had probably heard him and offered a lame excuse that his head ached constantly from the artillery rounds, his unit fired. I could tell that Anna's father was livid, but was holding his tongue."

Maggie also told me, "Anna desperately wants a child, but Christian wasn't interested in her. He just wants to drink his beer and yell about his headache. But regardless of how he treats her, she still wants his child. She's begged him, but he wouldn't do it. And then he told her that he doesn't ever want to bring a child into this world. How selfish he is. She sits and worries that he will be killed."

Just before Christmas, Christian reported to his artillery battalion, now in the newly formed 2nd Army. The Germans had insisted that their allies supply more manpower in Russia.

The newspapers reported on January 28th, 1942, *"The Einstazgruppen has completed a major operation against the Chetnik that started on January 4th. For 3 weeks, they searched through Novi Sad and surrounding villages for Serbs and Jews suspected of collaborating with the Chetnik guerillas. Nearly 4,000 were rounded up and brought to justice."*

It would be years later when I learned, that what was supposed to have been a police operation, was in fact mass murder. The most accurate count is that over 3,800 people were killed. At least two thirds of the dead were Serbs. I was shocked then, but hadn't known these facts at the time.

The newspapers read *"On April 11th, 1942, the 209,000man Hungarian 2nd Army deployed to Kursk in southern Russia. Advancing 120 miles, they reached the Don River on July 7th. There they manned a 200-kilometer sector south of Voronezh. Their mission is to protect the left flank of the German 6th Army and 4th Panzer Army during the attack on Stalingrad."*

Anna continued to pray for Christian.

"Konrad, I have a surprise for you. It's sure now. We're going to have a baby!" Maggie announced.

"Maggie, that's sure great news! Do you know when?"

"Maybe around Christmas, I think."

"Ha! A present for us. I'm hoping for a boy."

"We'll see. But that's what I want too."

When my sister, Terri, heard that Maggie was expecting she was thrilled. I heard Terri saying, "How are you feeling? Have you decided on names yet? Do you hope you'll deliver on Christmas?"

Maggie said, "You're lucky that your sons are too young to be dragged into this war." She regretted saying it as soon as the words left her mouth.

Terri's demeaner changed. We could see the fear in her. She said, "I pray all the time that the war will be over quickly and that they won't be old enough. I just don't know how I'll be able to handle it, if that falls on me."

I thought of Aunt Sophia, "What must it be like for her?" We didn't know, but by September, 1942, the 2nd Army had already had 30,000 casualties in fighting along the Don River. They were spread very thin. In some cases, there was only a forty-man platoon to cover a one-kilometer stretch of the front. We all prayed together for the safety of Sophia's boys.

In October, Stefan wrote, *"My Division has been deployed to southwest Serbia to fight the Chetnik guerillas. But within the ranks, we're having disciplinary problems with the Croats. Strict orders have been given not to make insults regarding their mothers. It escapes me, why that had become an issue for us.*

The Division has been declared a Mountain Division and equipped with good captured weapons like Czech machine guns and French light tanks. We also have excellent German-made mountain artillery. The fighting has been difficult in this terrain. Unfortunately, even with our best efforts, the Chetniks slipped through and retreated south into the mountains. But I'm happy with our victory and the opportunity to serve my country and fight against them."

He didn't say anything about the reprisals against the civilian population, but there were rumors brought by travelers from the south. We Hungarians killed 670 people, in gruesome mass murders and the burning of villages. These actions were clearly not within any accepted standards of warfare. But we weren't to learn, until months later, of the extent of these things.

When Maggie heard of it, she asked me, "Stefan wouldn't be involved in something like that, would he?"

I told her, "No. He's a good Catholic and knows better than to just kill people."

Magdalena was six months along and really showing. Many men were sending their families to Germany for safety.

"Maggie, what do you think about going to Germany with some of the other women and children? It would be safer for you and the baby and I'd worry a lot less."

"I will not! Not without you. If you feel that it isn't safe here in Apatin, then let's both go."

"But I wouldn't be surprised if they drafted me into the army when we got there. We would have to be ready to accept that."

"Then we're staying! I'm not going to let you get drafted and lose you. And I still don't think anyone will come here to find you. So, it's decided, we stay." She declared and she meant it.

December 17th, 1942 brought the birth of our son, Klein Mathias, named after my father of course. The "Klein" meaning

"Little" was to distinguish him from both my father, and Johann and Theresia's oldest son. He was a big boy at 4.35 kilograms, with a good healthy cry. There was nothing wrong with his appetite either. Maggie came through with no problems. We were even more blessed. I prayed to God with my thanks.

I decided that it was time to come back into public view and begin helping wait tables in the tavern. The past months had been so boring. One of the few books that I found was on business accounting. After easily digesting its contents I took over both the inn's and the bakery's accounting.

There wasn't much news about the battle at Stalingrad. Everything had gone silent. "No news is bad news." I thought to myself. The winter seemed particularly cold. Our future seemed uncertain.

2

THE INN AT APATIN

My parent's Inn, sat on the east bank of the Danube River. It had a wonderful view of the famous blue water and the boat traffic on it. The main building faced the river, about twenty feet above. A stairway with two levels ran down to a small docking facility along the riverbank.

If traveling from Belgrade north to Budapest, it was about halfway, and before reaching the old border with Hungary. If traveling from east to west, say from Arad, Romania to Zagreb, Croatia, it is also about halfway, and before crossing the Danube into Croatia.

Things didn't change much when Germany invaded Serbia and the border between Hungary and Serbia moved south.

Many travelers passed through the small village of Apatin, and with the number and variety of people, it was easy for smugglers to come and go without standing out. Hungary, Romania and Croatia all had more important things to worry about than chasing a few smugglers. Much went on, in our little Inn.

It was a three-story medieval-style structure. The walls were rough-cut stone for the first floor, stucco and lathe for the second and the roof's slate tiles made up the third. The first-floor dining room was at the south end, with a large fireplace at the middle of its end-wall. Then came the kitchen, and next the laundry/housekeeping area. And at the north end was the tavern. It also had a large fireplace at the middle of its end-wall. The street was on that side of the inn.

My father ran the tavern. He opened its outdoor patio in good weather. Patrons danced inside or out to local bands, many of whom were Roma. On different nights, they would play Hungarian, Croatian, Serbian or Swabian music. The Roma knew all the ethnic styles and could play tamburitza, citera, flute, zither, accordion, bagpipe, violin, gardon, clarinet, ta'rogato', hurdy-gurdy, verbunkos and cimbalom music. Each had its own fans.

The second-floor had twelve double guestrooms and the third floor twelve singles. Both floors had three rooms on each side of two hallways. The hallways ran from a central stairwell. Each room had its own toilet. Shower-rooms were at both ends of the second floor. One was for men and the other for the ladies. The shower-rooms had a fireplace for the comfort of the guests.

My father used the roof for his hobbies of breeding and racing carrier pigeons and operating a semaphore signal station. The station connected a site across the river in Croatia with a site further down the Danube. These stations were outmoded by radio, but were fun to keep up. For many years, they had been used to warn of approaching armies coming up or down the river.

The bakery was in a one-story building across the patio, at the street. Johann and Theresia worked long days running it. Their sons Mathias and Adam helped, after school and on summer vacation. They served coffee and pastries, cakes and breads at tables in their store or on the patio. They were open from early morning until the afternoon and then during the summer until the evening.

The dining room had a nice view south along the river. It consisted of six booths, three along each side wall, and six tables arranged in the center. Each sat four diners for a total capacity of forty-eight.

We were often booked to capacity at dinnertime. Hotel guests might have to share a booth or table with strangers. We tried our best to make compatible matches, but if the arrangement was not satisfactory, we offered to serve in the tavern or on the patio. For most we could work out an enjoyable seating.

The family—ten with the baby—lived in a two-story house behind the bakery. There was a tool shed in between. Our main meal was in the early afternoon. We ate what had been prepared to serve for our guests' evening meal.

Apatin was buzzing with the rumors in January, 1943. Could it be true? Was it possible that Germany had suffered such a great defeat? And Romania and Italy also? Were all three armies completely destroyed or captured? That was hard to believe.

And what had become of the Hungarian 2nd Army? No one was sure. Those with loved ones on the Don River waited in great anxiety and prayed. We all prayed with them.

Our receipts were paid in many currencies. We got: Hungarian Pengo"; Croatian Kroners; Serbian Dinars; Romanian Lei; German Marks; Slovakian Koruna; Swiss and French Francs; Italian Lira; British Pounds; and even some American Dollars. Using the daily newspaper, it was easy to keep up with the conversion rates. I did them in my head, when accepting payment. I was able to almost eliminate mistakes and that helped our profits.

We were using the local bank to convert to Pengo", when depositing into our account. That cost us the bank's fees on each transaction. "Why do that?" I reasoned. "Let's bundle and sell some of that currency to the smugglers for a small fee. They need the local currency where they buy. Or when they sell, in order to make change. Doing business in the local currency is always easier and less traceable by the authorities." Soon, a new and modestly profitable sideline began.

And I hid, as much as possible, of the Swiss Francs, English Pounds and American Dollars in the bakery's cold-room, in a can marked "Yeast".

Then a special delivery letter came for Aunt Sophia. It read:

We are sorry to give you bad news. Your sons, Ludwig Genser and Filipp Genser have been killed in fighting on the Don River. III Corps was cut off from 2nd Army. It then defended the

*German 2nd Army's flank, from 15 to 26 Jan. It ran short of
ammunition, and its anti-tank weapons were jammed by tem-
peratures as low as –45 ° C. Therefore, it retreated, in fog and
snow, through Soviet lines to the Olym River. We have reports
from eye-witnesses, that both your sons fought bravely until the
end. We have not been able to recover the bodies.*

Sophia screamed and collapsed in grief. It was terrible just to
witness her pain. There was nothing for her to even bury.

My mother never got over losing first her brother-in-law,
Michael, and now her nephews. She became withdrawn, stopped
running the front desk and stayed mostly in the house. Maggie
took over her responsibilities.

But Christian Theer managed to return to his home in Temerin
on February 28th. Anna greeted him with open arms and weeping
for joy. He could barely speak of his experiences. "I was lucky to
be behind the lines with my gun crew. Our guns kept freezing up
in the cold. That cold! Impossible! We just had to get out. So many
dead. It's still hard to imagine."

The newspaper read:

*Our Poor Brave Boys Come Home. Of the 209,000 men
in the 2nd Army only about 50,000 have returned to Hungary.
One third of those men are wounded. Most of the survivors were
rear echelon. It means that over 150,000 Hungarians were dead,
captured or missing on the frozen plains of the Ukraine. The
Battle of the Don River was the greatest catastrophe that the
Hungarian Army has ever suffered! Who is to blame?*

Sitting down to dinner together for the first time in over a
week, I asked, "Maggie, how are you and Little Matty today? Isn't
it his three-month birthday today? It's wonderful how big he's
getting. And it's wonderful to see you smiling."

"He's doing fine Konrad, and now so am I. I'm feeling much

better—not so depressed. Your mother and sister were such a big help to me. I was feeling so down. I didn't know what was wrong with me. But now that's over and I'm feeling better. But now there is this other thing happening. I'm worried now about our future here and Matty's. What will happen to us? Is it safe? Are the Russians going to come here?"

"They are still far away. I worry more about the Partisans slipping through and getting here, even this far north. But not Russians for now. For some other time...later...in the future, maybe. We need to work out a plan for that. We will have to be ready, able to move out quickly."

I thought to myself, *"This is a mess! What a way to try and raise a family. I have to find a way to protect them, if the worst happens. What do the smugglers know? How can I become friends with them? Or maybe a business partner? That would be even better. They will have ways to move quickly and through borders."*

Aunt Sophia came to me and asked, "You go to church all the time. Why do you think there's a God, when such terrible things happen? My husband and my sons are gone, and I'm left with nothing to even bury! Why would He be so cruel? I can't believe in God anymore."

"Sophie, I look at it this way. Think of all the people who have ever lived, the millions and millions. I don't know how many, but a lot going back through history. And what does God ask from all the people he made? I think it's love. And love requires the faith that He exists. You can't love something that you don't think exists."

And Sophie, "The bad things come from the Devil. It throws stuff at us to separate us from God. It is an ancient, very smart and very evil thing. It can easily fool humans. Why does God allow it to exist and do these bad things? To test us, and make us work hard to keep loving Him. That is the difference for those who will be with him after their tests are over, and we die. You have to keep loving and having faith."

"Nice words, Konrad, but a load of crap. See how it is for you when you start losing those that you really love."

"And Konrad, I want you to know something. I'm going to start making some money for myself. I'm going to, let's say, entertain the men who come to our Inn. I still have enough good looks to attract them. I need some of my own money and not just the room and board and tips that I pick up serving food. I want nice things and to have money enough to live on when I'm old. You shouldn't deny me that or have a problem. Right?"

"Sophie, I don't know if that's the right thing for you. Can you handle all the bad things that come with something like that?"

"It's not for you to say—to try and lead my life for me. I think that it will be fun, and if not, I can just stop. But I don't see why it should be a problem. I always found that stuff very enjoyable."

"It's just that I never thought of you that way! Please keep it discrete, so that our business isn't driven away. We can't afford a bad reputation. But while you're doing it, please stay alert for any opportunities for me. I need to get some kind of business going with one or two smugglers. This family needs an escape plan, if the Russians show up here. The smugglers will have the best escape routes and the most experience."

She did a good job with that. Not long after, the dining room was emptying out after dinner. Sophie came in and sat with two guests that I hadn't seen before. One waved me over to their table. I thought they wanted to order desert or a drink or something.

One said, "Come, sit with us. Sophie here told us to see you. I'm Josip and my friend here is Draza. Have a drink with us. We have a proposition for you."

I could tell that Josip was Serbian and Draza, Croatian. That was a strange combination to be having dinner with each other.

I sat and he went on, "Sophie told us about your business. That you are always looking at ways to make money for your family." And in a low voice, "And that you convert money to different currencies. Can you convert Dinars to Lei?"

"Yeah. Sure. How much?" I said.

Josip said, "With the defeat at Stalingrad and collapse of Romania's Army, Draza now has new German MG42 machine guns for sale. They are stored across the river in Croatia waiting for buyers. They come six to a crate with replacement barrels included. Cost to me is two hundred fifty thousand Lei per crate."

"That's a lot for me, even for just one crate. But if you give me a week it would be ninety-five thousand Dinars with my fee."

"We don't want to wait around. How about a hundred thousand Dinars if you get us the Lei by Thursday. That's 2 days, and after that going down a thousand for every day beyond."

Draza smiled a thin smile that wasn't really a smile, and said, "The first time, is always the toughest." I wasn't sure of his meaning.

Josip said, "We can come back every other week for the same deal."

"That sounds like too much for me to handle. But the profit is really nice. So, I'll try." Draza said, "Now that you know our business, you should try real hard. If you're not our partner, then you're our problem. Josip is with the Partisans and can't afford for you to have loose lips."

"I told you that I'd try and I will. But there are no promises. And I don't talk about my business to anyone. So, you have no worries there."

It was a difficult choice for me, since Stefan was fighting Serbians and these guns could be used against him and his men. On the other side of the coin, not only could we make a lot of money, but these guys were just what I wanted. They would be our guarantee of a way to escape if the Russians showed up.

"I'll be back with the hundred thousand Dinars. Don't forget or anything. Two hundred fifty thousand Lei by Thursday evening. No funny business. We know who you are and where your family is. If we get robbed, arrested or killed, you will have visitors."

Aunt Sophie smiled at me. *"What kind of a smile was that?"* I wondered.

But I had bigger fish to fry. I said to myself, *"Think Konrad, think! Loan shark? Parents? Relative? Bank loan? Friends? Enemies? Business acquaintances? Some combination? All of them had their problems. There should be about half between our bank account and the "Yeast" can, but most of it isn't in Lei.*

After Josip and Draza left, Sophie said, "You have a problem? Heh? Well, I have a solution. But we need to be equal partners. Or I don't bother to help you out."

"What's your solution then, Sophie?"

She said, "I've spent none of the money that the government has given me as Michael's widow for the last twenty-two months. Or for Ludwig and Filipp for the last three months. I just didn't want to touch it. Blood Money! Plus, I've earned some money here, doing what I told you. And, Stefan has been sending me money to save for him. His mother won't touch it. She knows what he's doing. Plus, Christian has been more than generous, as he wants things that he can't get at home. Add it all up and it's a little more than a half of what we need. Do you have anything saved?"

I told her, "I've saved some also, but it's in Swiss Francs, English Pounds and American Dollars. They would be harder to convert to Lei without being noticed. But if I did convert that money, it should be enough for the other half."

So, she proposed, "Let's be partners. I can go to the bank and convert everything that isn't Lei already. The bank manager is a client of mine, so it won't be a problem. And their fee will be in trade. We go 50/50 on this business? Deal? And we can do more together in the future." And she gave me that same smile again.

I took Sophie's deal and we had the two hundred fifty thousand Lei ready for Josip when he came down for dinner on Thursday. "Well this is a pleasant surprise. I was worried about you. Here is the hundred thousand Dinars. You've proved yourself to be reliable, so you won't see Draza again. I'll be back, in two or three weeks. Keep a good thought for me."

Every time he visited us, Sophie and I would split the profit of thirteen-hundred and sixty-eight Pengo'. Of course, it varied over time with the exchange rates, but it was around that for quite a while. That part of the deal worked great for everyone.

Out-of-the-blue, Sophie was now making a different problem for me. "Sophie! Be careful! I'm a married man." I was resisting, but she wanted more than just a business partnership.

"You've seen one of these before. And from what I can tell, you're enjoying the view."

"Cut it out and let's talk business."

"Oh, okay, Konrad. I was just thinking. It's risky for us to keep this much of our assets in Lei and not in some rock-solid currency like Swiss Franks or Pounds. I think that Josip and Draza would also see the benefit of transacting at least part that way, in such a currency. You should talk to Josip about it so that none of us have all our eggs in one basket."

"Yes, that's a good idea and I'll try to convince Josip to talk to Draza on his next swing."

"But, come on. You're so cute. We could also have some fun together."

"No, Sophie, no!

Soon the switch was made to half Pounds and half Lei. Sophie and I combined our profits and saved our Pounds together in the "Yeast" can.

We kept our working funds separate in the tool shed. The packet—one hundred twenty-five thousand Lei and one hundred seventy-five Pounds—was kept in a can marked, "Danger—Rat Poison". The shed was padlocked. There were only two keys. Sophie and I each had one.

3

STEFAN'S FURLOUGH

One morning, while preparing my guest invoices, I heard, "Hello Konrad." Looking up I was surprised to see Stefan standing there. In fact, shocked might be a better word, as the details of his dark green dress uniform came into focus.

It had golden yellow epilates indicating his rank of Hauptleute (Captain); an SS patch on his lower left sleeve; 7th SS Mountain Division shoulder patch on the upper sleeve; collar patch indicating gehobener dienst (elevated school level, but with no college degree); and Iron Cross First Class medal worn on his left breast, meaning he had accomplished two heroic actions in battle. A different looking pistol was on his hip, now in an open, faster access holster.

At a glance, everyone, whether local or visitor, would know exactly what he was. And a non-Reich German didn't advance in the SS ranks, unless he was an enthusiastic volunteer. Most Swabians weren't volunteers, so were held in distain, by the German officers. Everyone would be certain then, just based on these things, that his service was purposeful. And, in addition, he was a war hero. He would be feared and hated by many people around here.

"Hello Stefan! What a surprise! What are you doing home? Did you travel all night?"

"Don't you want to see me, Konrad?"

A cold feeling ran through me. "Of course, I want to see you. It's just a surprise, out of the blue and everything."

But my thoughts were on Josip, who was due in at any time. *"How to keep the two separated? That would be a trick."*

Then I said, "Mother and Father will be so happy to see you."

"Maybe Father, but I don't think Mother. She stopped answering my letters last year."

"Yes, I know. Father said something. But I didn't press Mother for an explanation. It was over the rumors, right?"

"Exactly what rumors, Konrad."

It wasn't good, that this was coming to a head so quickly, but there was no way around it. "About the 7th SS Mountain Division massacring civilians. Those rumors!" I said it, and now it was out in the open.

Stefan paused and looked me in the eyes. "You haven't experienced war, so it's hard to explain to you. My soldiers, the men I'm responsible for, are dying, in ways that aren't battle against a uniformed foe. We see our comrades killed, by what seconds ago appeared to be an innocent civilian. It is so hard to tell who is trying to kill you. The lines get blurred. We have our orders. And we only have each other out there. We don't forget our comrades that have been lost. And everyone has learned to hate. So sometimes things get crazy. They get out of control. It spins into something that can only be described as ugly. But I came home to try and forget, at least for two weeks. Can you give me that? Do we need to talk about this anymore?"

There were many ways to respond, but none of them seemed right. Finally, I said, "Yes of course. You need this time with us. Come to the house and relax for a little." And to change the subject, "What kind of pistol is that? It looks different."

"It's a new issue for us, a Walther. Very reliable. I carry it with me all the time now, even when I'm out of uniform." He pulled it out and showed it to me, but kept it in his hand.

The house seemed empty when we went in. The boys were at school and Mother didn't answer my call. "I'll tell everyone that you're here. We'll all get together in a few hours at dinner. Don't worry. You will see, that everyone is happy that you're home, if even for a short time."

"Maggie, I have a surprise for you." Maggie was at the front desk with Little Matty next to her, sleeping in his pram. "Stefan is home. You will see him at dinner in a little while."

"Oh, damn! I can't go to him right now. The front desk can't be empty when quests are checking out. And I don't have anything special prepared. How is he? How does he look? Is he okay? Tell him how I'm tied up here and that I'll be over as soon as I can."

"He's changed, tired looking. And scary, the way his eyes look and how he carries himself with that pistol on his hip. He's still Stefan, but different. But I can't explain how. You'll see for yourself. But he's still committed to what he's doing, from the way he talks."

"Oh, poor guy. I'll have to prepare his favorites. I'll start a hasenpfeffer for three days from now, stuffed peppers tomorrow and sauerbraten for in between. Our guests at the Inn will think that we're rich."

"You've always spoiled him, but that's good now. He needs us, for him to get his head straight." But Josip's shadow hung over everything that I was saying.

I went to tell Father, who was in the tavern preparing for the evening. The tavern was empty except for him. "Father, Stefan is home."

"Where is he? I must congratulate him. He has made me so proud. We Hungarians must keep those Serb bastards at bay. And he's the hero doing it. But I better be careful that there's no Serbs around now, who could hear me. We can't afford to lose any business."

"He's in the house. I told him to rest for a few hours until dinner. He looked very tired. Why don't you wait until then?"

"Oh, okay. I'll wait. Did he see Mother?"

"I don't think she was there. The house seemed empty. I called out to her, but there was no answer."

"She's there alright. Where else would she be? You know that she never leaves the house anymore. Probably saw you coming, recognized him and hid in the bedroom. Locked the door. She doesn't want to see him. Thinks what he's doing is sinful. The priest told her not to even give him a hug or a kiss."

"I called to her, but didn't go searching."

When Mathias and Adam came in from school in midafternoon, we gathered for a dinner of sausage and red cabbage. Maggie had nursed Klein Matty and put him down for his nap. Father, myself, Maggie, Johann, Terri, Sophie, and the boys sat around the table waiting for Stefan. But no Mother.

When he came down the stairs everyone cheered. He had changed to casual cloths and even in the few hours looked more rested and like his old self. There were hugs, handshakes, kisses and tears before everyone finally settled down to eat.

At the end of the meal, Stefan said, "I'm sorry that Mother didn't join us. I'd like to see her, of course. Please tell her that I love her and that I'd like to talk. Maybe we can break the ice, work things out."

I never heard if anyone raise the question of the rumors with Stefan. Things went along like that for about a week. Mother hadn't budged. As far as I know she did not see her son.

At night Stefan enjoyed the music and dancing in the tavern. Then early one evening, unexpectedly, Josip was there. He waved me over to his stool. After the hellos he asked, "Who is that?" indicating Stefan, "And why is he armed?" The pistol was clearly visible on Stefan's hip.

"That's just my brother. Don't worry about him. He's okay."

"I haven't seen him before. Is he just visiting? Those Walthers are new and hard to get. Does he have a connection? Maybe we could work out a deal and I could buy some from you?"

"I don't think that he has any connections."

"Bring your brother over and let me ask him."

"That wouldn't be a good idea. I don't want any trouble in here."

And with that, I could see that Josip's emotions changed quickly for the worse. Becoming angry, he reached down, lifted his pants leg and pulled something from his sock. He got up from the stool. I quickly put myself between them. My back was to Stefan, but he must have seen the sudden movement.

I heard him say, "Is there a problem, Konrad?"

"Come join us", Josip called around me, but I knew that was a ruse.

Father said from behind the bar, "Hey Serb! Get out! We want no trouble makers in here." And he waved the sawed-off pool cue that he kept behind the bar. He had years of experience with ejecting trouble-makers.

"Just a little misunderstanding, Father. I can work this out. Everyone please calm down."

Josip gave it a long thought, and said, "Okay, let's talk then." He sat back down on his stool and pocketed whatever had been in his hand. "What is your brother's name?"

"Stefan." I answered.

Father put the pool cue back and said, "Okay. Let's have some music!" he yelled to the band. And it seemed to be over.

Josip yelled, "Hey brother Stefan! Let me buy you a drink. Come on over. No problems. I give my word." I relaxed a bit. Stefan made his way over.

"Stefan, this is Josip. He's a friend and business associate of mine. He's a nice guy. You'll like him."

"Or at least not kill him", I earnestly hoped to myself.

They had beers together and made small talk. The music enveloped the room. It was a calming influence. Everything seemed fine. Then Josip brought up the Walther again.

"Those Walthers are new. Hard to get. Where did you get yours?"

"I'm am officer in the 7ᵗʰ SS Mountain Division. I'm home on leave for two weeks. Can't wait to get back to my men. I'll be going back in two days."

"You didn't tell me, Konrad, that your brother was fighting in Serbia. Brave man. A hero for Hungary. I could give Stefan a few leads in fighting the Partisans. Communist bastards that they are."

"Stefan, where is your unit right now?" Josip asked.

"Everyone knows that we are in Mostar being resupplied, but I won't learn our new orders until I get back. Who knows? There are no fixed battle lines down there. But soon. I've been ordered not to be late getting back."

Even with only that, Stefan had said too much and Josip took it all in. They spoke for another hour, before Stefan retired for the night. Then Josip and I finished our business for this trip. Both he and Stefan would be leaving in one more day. Stefan south to Mostar, and Josip across the river to Croatia. Then I could relax.

On the next day, Sunday, it was time to attend the 8:00 AM Mass at The Assumption of Blessed Virgin Mary Catholic Church in the center of town. Six of us went including Mother, the two Diplich boys (Mathias and Adam), Maggie, Klein Matty and myself. Johann and Theresia were working at the bakery as usual.

Father, Aunt Sophie and Stefan chose to spend the morning eating pastries, drinking coffee and smoking cigarettes on the patio.

At dinner, Maggie's hasenpfeffer was a hit. Anna and Christian Theer and Mr. Roth traveled to join us and see Stefan before he returned to the fighting. We did not discuss the war or politics, but rather just enjoyed each other's company and the fine Spring weather. It was a day whose memory would have to last us a long time. But Mother had not joined us and Mr. Roth was bruised from "taking a fall". Stefan made his goodbyes that night.

Maggie and I saw him off early the next morning. Josip was not far behind him, but in the opposite direction. It was back to normal, but my worries about the course of the war were constantly increasing as I read each day's newspaper.

In mid-June, I received a letter from Stefan. He was in the hospital in Sarajevo. The letter read:

> *Dear Konrad,*
>
> *Please tell everyone that I'm doing fine now. I'm recovering at this military hospital from my wounds. I'm out of danger, but the bad news is that my left leg was amputated below the knee.*
>
> *My Company was part of two battalions moved to the Sutjeska River to block the Partisans' escape. We had established ourselves near the little village of Tjentiste.*
>
> *A large force of them attacked at night. It was like they knew our positions. I understand now that there were four battalions from their 1st Dalmatian and 5th Montenegro Brigades. We were outnumbered, caught by surprise and forced to retreat in order to regroup.*
>
> *I'm extremely proud of my men for what followed. In nighttime, hand-to-hand fighting we recovered our positions and really laid into them. Our training and disciple came to the forefront. In short, our enemy was brave but out of their element in large force fighting and maneuvering.*
>
> *As we were attacking, what I feel was a lucky shot shattered my lower leg. My medics were able to get a tourniquet on it and I stayed with the men until passing out. Unfortunately, the leg could not be saved. But I'm much better off than many of the men here. It was a costly battle.*
>
> *It's my hope to be discharged soon. The doctors and nurses have been great and treated me like some sort of celebrity. I still have some rehab work to do to help with my walking. Then I can come home. Please remember me in your prayers. My best to everyone.*
>
> *Stefan*

I shared the letter with everyone in the family and got different, but not surprising reactions. Stefan was everyone's hero except for Mother. She nodded that she understood, but said nothing. I think that by this point she had stopped thinking of Stefan as her son.

I couldn't help but wonder if Stefan had let slip too much to Josip, when they were drinking in the tavern. Or if the machine-guns that we were helping send to the Partisans had been used in the battle. I would never know the answer to either.

Around that time, the losses from the Don River fighting last winter were being fully felt by families all over Hungary. The dead, wounded, captured and missing soldiers were being grieved or prayed for by many, if not most, families.

The people felt that enough was enough and that Hungary should ask for an armistice. While the government couldn't come out and say, it certainly seemed like Hungary was already doing that. There was minimal bombing from the western air-forces. Everyone, including Germany, guessed that talks had already been started. On August 9th, the papers announced an armistice.

Stefan returned home on August 13th. He was in full uniform and the medal he wore was the *Order of the German Cross in Gold*. That medal was awarded for continuous bravery before the enemy or excellence in commanding troops. Its distinguishing feature was the large black swastika in its middle. It was awarded to very few non-Reich Germans.

Later, when we had a chance to talk, he said to me, "I wonder now if it was all worth it. The death and destruction that I saw was terrible. My men were so angry after the battle. Before they took me to the hospital, I saw prisoners being killed. I wanted to go and stop it, but couldn't get up. I think that it will haunt me all my life. What do you think, Konrad? Do you think I should have gone off to this war at all? Losing the leg doesn't bother me. I got off easy in that respect. It's the things in my mind. Was I right to go? Was I evil?"

"Stefan, you should see a priest. I can't answer those things for you. Pray and go to Confession. That's the best for you. Your family loves you. And Mother will come around. Give her time. She loves you. But if I were you, I wouldn't wear the uniform again, at least for now. You need to come back to civilian life. You need to forget and try to come home in your mind."

"I'm going to try to do that."

But the question was, would the world let him.

After the war ended, it would be written:

Everything they came across was burnt down, they murdered and pillaged. The officers and men of the SS division Prinze Eugen committed crimes of outrageous cruelty on this occasion. The victims were shot slaughtered and tortured, or burnt to death in burning houses. Where a victim was found not in his house but on the road or in the fields some distance away he was murdered and burnt there. Infants with their mothers, pregnant women and frail old people were also murdered. In short, every civilian met with by these troops in these villages was murdered. In many cases, whole families who, not expecting such treatment or lacking the time to escape, had remained quietly in their homes were annihilated and murdered. Whole families were thrown into burning houses in many cases and thus burnt. It has been established from the investigations entered upon that 121 persons, mostly women and including 30 persons aged 60-92 years and 29 children of ages ranging from six months to 14 years, were executed on this occasion in the horrible manner narrated above. The villages were burnt down and razed to the ground.

Dr. Dusan Nedeljkovic, Yugoslav State Commission, Document D-940

These things had happened right after Stefan was wounded and hospitalized.

"Maggie, we need to talk. What do you think about the odds that Hungary will surrender and then whether German troops will come here and take over?"

"Do you think that could happen, Konrad? Oh, my God! They'll want all the men and even the boys. Where could we go? Who would we leave behind? What would Stefan do?"

4

LUDWIG'S WAR

"Fil, wake up!" Ludwig slapped him hard so that he would move.

"Huh. Okay. I'm awake."

"Shush. You were snoring so loud. Be quiet. I thought I heard someone moving around a minute ago. Russians, maybe, I think. Lay still and be quiet."

For the next five minutes Ludwig peered over the edge of the icy rut they were lying in. A rut made by someone's tank, a while ago and before the freezing set in. Thick fog blanketed everything. He heard nothing. Saw nothing except fog, which seemed to never lift.

"There's no one around. We can talk. I'm so cold. How are you doing?"

No response.

"Fil, wake up!"

"Huh. Yeah, right."

"Fil, count your ammo."

"I just did that a few minutes ago."

"That was an hour ago."

"What's the difference, Lud? It's still the same."

"The difference is that you need to stay awake. Count your ammo again and tell me."

"Two full clips, so twenty there and about a half clip in my rifle. So around twenty-five. But my rifle keeps jamming. Just like everyone else's did when we were attacked."

"I know, Fil. These Gewehr 41s are so finicky. They foul-up so quickly. And when they foul-up, it's like just having a bolt-action.

It really slows down getting shots off. But mine is working fine and I have three clips plus a full one loaded, so forty overall for me."

"Do you think that there's any chance of finding one of our units and maybe even getting a meal? I'd love some food right about now!"

"Stop dreaming. Have you ever seen cold like this? It seems like an enemy all by itself. Damn river was frozen solid. They just walked across it. Some defensive barrier the Don River turned out to be. They were on us like that." Ludwig snapped his fingers. "And so many of them. They just kept coming and it seemed like only our század (company) was there to stop them. You and I were lucky to be a little separated from the rest. They went right over them. Now it's like we've been swallowed up by this place. All alone and it's so vast and we're so isolated."

"Our század was spread out over a mile. Once it turned cold, even communication with the other units was impossible. How many times did the batteries for our radios die? And how many times did the damned motorcycles freeze to the ground? And even when we got them free, it was impossible for them to move in the ice and snow. Somebody wasn't thinking!"

Ludwig again looked over the edge. Now he could vaguely see the dark shape of the trees below. He thought, "They seem to be looming, dangerous, hiding their secrets and maybe the enemy. They are frightening, not friendly trees. Maybe I should just stay in this rut and sleep. No, I'm not going to give in to that. And I won't leave my brother behind either. We have to move right now or this is where we'll die."

Fil, are you with me? Fil!"

"Huh, yeah. I'm here."

"We have to move. Now! Let's go before we freeze to death."

They staggered downhill to a little frozen creek.

They began following it up-stream, away from the Don.

"Fil, what does your compass say?"

"Northwest."

"Good, mine too. Keep moving. Hear that fighting off to our right. Sounds like maybe five kilometers. Let's hope that it's drawn all the Russians that way."

"Yeah, maybe we'll be lucky."

Zap. Thunk. Crack. A round passed and hit a tree behind them. They hit the ground and lay still.

"What's the password?"

A pause.

"What's the damn password, before we start shooting for real?"

"Mountain-storm!" Fil yelled back.

"Advance. Real slow, with your rifles over your heads."

They followed their orders.

"Open your parkas and let me see your uniforms."

They did, as they continued to move forward.

"I'm Captain Bauer, század commander. Which platoon . . . ? Oh, it's the Genser twins. Good to see that you made it."

"Aren't you afraid that the Russians will hear you shooting?"

"Shots being fired all around here. One shot isn't going to attract much attention."

"Do you have any food? We're hungry and cold."

"We only have a few rations. Eat fast, a little now, and put some in your pockets. We have to move out, so don't take long."

There were ten of them. Captain Bauer told them, "Spread out. Walk single file, with five meters between. We're going up-stream to the northwest. Do not speak! And that's an order."

The fog limited their vision, but also protected them from discovery. The cold was like a knife slicing through even their winter uniforms. It made men want to give up, to not want to live to fight another day.

They pressed on toward the Hungarian lines, not knowing how far back their army had retreated. Near the end of the day, they left the stream-bed, when it meandered south. They climbed a hill, and stopped. The wind had finally cleared the fog enough, so that below they could make out an encamped infantry company. By the look of their quilted uniforms, they were Russians.

"I'm afraid that we didn't make it boys." Captain Bauer said as they huddled around him. "The way that I see it, if we stay out here overnight, or if we try to go back, we'll all just freeze to death. If we try to go around, we'll surely get caught, and die running, with our backs to the enemy. So, it's attack and die like soldiers, or surrender and hope that they don't just kill us. Anyone have anything to say before I decide?"

"If we surrender, do you think they'll feed us?" Fil said.

"How the hell do I know?" said the Captain. "That decides it. We attack! Sargent, do you think that you can sneak up on a sentry and put him out of commission?"

"Yeah. No problem. My pleasure."

"Okay the rest of us will fan out, two meter separation and when the sentry goes down, we'll try for that large tent in the center. It probably has the communications and officers in there. Any questions?"

No one said a word. Their training took over. They fanned out and with the Sargent ahead by ten meters. They slowly and stealthily crawled down the hill. It took them fifty minutes to make the two-hundred-meter crawl.

As he crawled, Ludwig had time to think of death and what happened after. He thought, "Death is welcome to me now, and Jesus will surely welcome me if I'm brave and do my duty. I just hope it is quick and not too painful. I'll find out soon enough and anyway this damned cold will end. At least I'll go with honor as a soldier. Shit, it's cold."

The Sargent was well trained, and experienced, so his kill went without detection. They rose and rushed forward toward the tent. As soon as the first shots were fired, the camp came alive. Some of them had their rifles foul. Some ran out of ammo and fixed bayonets, to fight as trained. They killed fifteen enemy soldiers but failed to reach the tent. Six of them were killed. The four remaining were surrounded and out of ammunition, forced to surrender.

Ludwig was among the four who surrendered. But Filipp wasn't. And Ludwig didn't have much time to think about the loss of his twin brother. He raised his hands in surrender when his ammo ran out. "You'll pay, Kraut bastard." This was all he remembered hearing before the rifle butt came down on his head. He woke the next morning, being tossed into the bed of a truck.

There were eight of them, either unwounded or just slightly wounded. He was on the truck all that day, but remembered little, passed out most of the times. He regained consciousness when they reached a small railroad station. The sign said "Chertkovo". He had no idea where that was. There they and the other captured Hungarian soldiers were fed a thin cabbage soup, before being ordered into boxcars.

Ludwig cried and thought, "How will I get along now without my brother? There will be no one like him for me ever again. My best friend. How will I tell my mother? I saw him get shot and then lying there dead in the snow. Why wasn't it me?"

Someone shouted, "Does anyone know where we're headed?" There was no answer. There were over sixty men in the boxcar, but no senior officers. Before the junior officers and enlisted men were loaded, the more seriously wounded and the senior officers had been separated from them.

After the train left, all the senior officers and the wounded were marched or carried into the woods and machine-gunned. Then any, still showing signs of life, were shot in the back of the head. They were left there on the ground to rot. But Ludwig was unaware of these things.

The boxcars had three vertical layers of wooden platforms for sleeping. They stopped four times during the trip, Lipetsk, Moskva, Yaroslavl and Kotlas. The men were ordered off and fed at the end of each day.

In the late afternoon of the fifth day, the train pulled into a small station named "Ukhta", in the Komi Republic and screeched to a halt. They got off again, and after being fed, climbed onto Studebaker trucks from America. Crossing a river by ferry, they traveled on an unpaved road, through the thick evergreen forest.

Many of the "settlers", who had come there in the early years of the 20th century, were prisoners of the Gulag, sent by the hundreds of thousands to perform forced labor in the Arctic region. Labor-camps, were carved out of the untouched forests by these "settlers".

Now these Gulags were almost empty due to starvation this winter. The rapid Axis advances had caused disastrous food shortages. Lumber production was essential and the USSR was experimenting with the use of Eastern European prisoners, to fill the depleted ranks. But not Ukrainians, who were shot immediately when captured. They were considered as traitors to the USSR.

On the second day of driving, the they reached their final destination. They were at one of the forcedlabor camp sites. About half of the twenty-five thousand Hungarians captured in the Battle of the Don were sent to this site in the Ural Mountains. Here they would cut timber in a seemingly endless boreal forest of pines, spruces and larches. Only the physically and mentally strong would survive until the end of the war.

"Line up, you bastards! Everyone line-up and come to attention! I am your unit leader. Leader of the new H Company. There is one letter of our alphabet, the Russian alphabet, for each Company in this Brigade. You are in H Company. H is the fifteenth letter of our alphabet. Each Company has its own barracks area. Except for work, you will never under any circumstances leave your barracks area.

We have twenty-five work-gangs in our Company. Each is assigned a number. Each work-gang has twenty men. Each man is assigned a number. You will no longer use your name or rank. To be identified you will use your two-digit number, followed by

4 LUDWIG'S WAR   35

your two-digit work-gang number, followed by H. For example, one of you will be 1607H.

You will address me as "Comrade" or more formally as "Comrade Peter". I am with the Main Administration for the Affairs of POWs and Internees of the GUPVI. We are in charge of all work-camps like this one.

I hope that you understand these two instructions, because failure to comply will result in your death."

And Ludwig thought, "If I can survive my unit being over-run, then that damned cold, and then that attack where everyone figured they'd die, then I can survive this and live to go home, even if that takes a long time. This will not break me. Nothing will." His new name was 0915H.

H Company lived in five barracks-buildings arranged in a "U" shape with two for either side and one for the bottom. There were five work-gangs to each. An assembly ground was in the center. Each morning they would report there before marching out into the forest to the day's work site. Comrade Peter's small home was at the open end.

Ludwig's group of one-hundred prisoners made up the five work-gangs that occupied the barracks at the bottom of the "U" — Barracks C. Their daily food ration did not have enough calories to sustain all the men, in view of their workload and the Arctic cold.

The stronger men formed gangs and took extra, in order to survive. The weaker, non-gang members, did not last long. More non-German — Polish, Hungarian, Romanian, Italian and Croatian — prisoners were always available to fill the ranks here, so the Russians didn't care, as long as the supply of lumber was uninterrupted.

Ludwig thought, "I was lucky to be assigned to a new company, to get in on the ground floor." His gang was led by 0615H. Right after they arrived 06, as Ludwig called him, was quick to surround himself with the smartest men he could find.

The six gang members worked together, formed lasting friend-ships and had each other's back.

The work was hard, but they paced themselves and mus-cled-up as the first weeks went by. If anything, Comrade Peter seemed pleased, and even a bit amused.

Long term, such arrangements helped keep the output of lumber steady.

"We have a problem with that new one, 1212H. First did you see the size of him. And smart too. Trying to form his own gang and take over our barracks. The sooner that we deal with him the better. Got any ideas for that 09?"

"We need a timely accident. That would be best. Let me see what I can come up with. I'll think of something, 06."

A few hours later, "I've got it! Let's go to Comrade Peter and get 1212 reassigned to work-gang 25. You know, the one that keeps the road open from the cutting and loading area to the train depot. Those roads are constantly iced and very difficult to drive. Comrade Peter will do it, if we can convince him that 1212 would be prefect due to his strength. And the trucks are always sliding around. What do you think, 06?"

"Do we know any drivers, who we could bribe?"

"I don't, but maybe one of our other guys does. But before we bribe one, we should get Comrade Peter to make the switch. It's sort of a 'chicken-or-egg' problem, whether we get the driver first or get the switch done first. But I think it will be better to go to Comrade Peter first.

And even if we don't get a driver, 1212H might be killed on that job anyway, run down in a real accident. And did you hear that there might be a tiger out there? More than one guy has just disappeared. First, let's just get him out there and then we'll see what we can do."

"Okay. Sounds good. Let's go and see the Comrade after we eat tonight."

Comrade Peter held up his hand indicating that they should

stop talking. "Let me have my dinner in peace. I like this idea and will take care of it tomorrow. I've heard from others that 1212H is a problem and this is the best solution that has been presented to me. I just hope that he doesn't freeze to death, get hit by a truck or even get eaten by a tiger. Yes, the tigers are there and they've eaten prisoners. We've known that for a number of months. Two tigers we think. But who knows? Right?" And he laughed.

As they were leaving the Comrade's house, 06 said, "Well that was easy. He just wants the lumber to keep flowing and doesn't need a troublemaker around to screw that up. Now to find a driver, 09. I'll leave that to you."

1212H became 1525H the next day and began working out on the road to the train depot. Many thought that he was an unlucky man. On his third day working on the road, he was hit and killed by a skidding truck.

0915H still hadn't found a driver, so it was either an accident plain and simple, or someone else wanted him dead and made the arrangements. Everyone in the gang thought that it was Comrade Peter, but no one was going to ask.

After the Fall harvest in 1943, the food supply in the USSR improved. And as a result, the rations in the camp improved. Everyone, including the replacement prisoners, were now fed properly. And lumber production increased, as there were fewer inexperienced workers.

5

JOHANN THE BAKER

"My name is Johann Diplich. My wife Theresia and I own the bakery business in Apatin. This is the way that I remember my experiences, starting in the Summer of 1943."

I smiled, looking over the counter at the stranger.

"You're next. What would you like this beautiful Sunday morning?" It wasn't unusual for guests from the Inn to start the day with a pastry and coffee from my bakery.

"One of those Italian looking things and a black coffee." he said pointing into the glass counter.

With his Serbian accent, now I recognized this man. I thought, *"Ah, Konrad's and Sophia's customer! I know Sophia's business with him, but not Konrad's. But he keeps coming back every few weeks. So that's a good thing."*

But there was no smile from the man in return. He went out and sat at one of the tables on the patio. First Sophia and then Herr Butscher, Konrad's father, joined him. Sophia came in and ordered three coffees and two crullers. She took them back to the table without volunteering anything about the meeting.

"A wonderful early-summer day, isn't it?" My curiosity had gotten the better of me and I went out and stood at the table.

"It was okay until you stuck your nose in our conversation", the Serbian said.

After bussing one of the tables in order to cover my anger, I went back inside. I was mumbling to myself, "Who doesn't like the baker? Everyone loves the baker! And who didn't like an early summer day's bright sunshine? Everyone likes sunshine! And who is so grumpy, that they won't chat? Someone who Konrad and Sophia would bring around to my business! That's who."

"What did you say, dear?" my wife, Theresia, said. She was inside waiting on customers.

"What do you think they're up to, those three?"

"Why do you think that they are up to something, Johanie?"

"Well last month Father Butscher waived a pool cue at him in the tavern and now there they are with their heads together, cooking something up and acting very secretive."

"Just forget it and help me with the customers."

"Okay, but, I know they're up to something. I just don't know if it's important."

The rest of the day went along in an uneventful way. Our boys came home from Mass around 11 AM. Mathias, was now seventeen, and Adam, a year younger. Mathias was scheduled to graduate from school next year.

"Stop that fooling around, and start your chores. We've had a busy day and there's a lot for you to do here", Theresia told them in a stern voice.

Mathias had been adopted after we tried for what seemed like forever, praying that God would give us a child. Then Adam came along almost immediately after that. "It's funny how that works. But our prayers were answered! What good boys!"

It was just a few days later, in June, 1943, when Stefan's letter arrived, telling us about his being wounded, during the battle at Tjentiste. In return, we all him sent letters and offered prayers for his speedy recovery.

Our Regent, Vice-Admiral Miklos Horthy had earned great prestige by re-establishing the Hungarian Kingdom after World War I. But in June 1941 he was persuaded to commit Hungary to the Axis alliance. But our losses on the Don River turned the populace against the war.

Then the newspapers reported that Hungary agreed to an armistice on August 9th, 1943. I thought, "Thank God for that.

We are not prepared for more suffering and losses like that, from fighting with the Russians. But we are also committed by this agreement to stop fighting in Serbia. I'm not sure about that. The Serbs want to come back up the Danube and take back our homeland. They will not be kind to us Swabians."

On August 13th, Stefan returned home. He put away his uniform and began trying to adjust to civilian life. He told me that he wondered if it had all been a mistake for him to go to Serbia. He said, "Konrad and I agreed that I should see a priest."

I told him, "That's a good idea for you. You've done your duty and need to put the fighting behind you. God will forgive you if you confess your sins." I thought to myself, "But probably not the Serbians."

A couple of days later, it was reported that Stefan's, 7th SS Division Prinz Eugen, was being sent to the Dalmatian coast to disarm the Italian forces there. Italy had just surrendered completely to the Allies. In September and October, the 7th SS successfully fought the Partisans in battles for control of that coast.

"I guess the Germans can't count on Hungarian units fighting in Serbia itself any longer. But who will stop the Partisans from coming here now?"

"Johann, come and sit with us!" Sophie waved and invited me. It was a Sunday morning in October and she was with her Serbian and Herr Butscher again. They had ordered their coffees and pastries about thirty minutes earlier and were conspiring since then.

"What do you think will happen around here in the next few months?" the Serbian said as I sat down. "By the way, my name is Josip."

"If you mean with the war, I don't know, but everyone loves the baker. So, we, my family and I, will be safe. My name is Johann."

"So, when the artillery shells come in a year or so from now, you'll wave a croissant at them?"

"We want you to think seriously about what you, and your

wife and boys will do when the Serbs come up the river. It's important that we know now, so that arrangements can be made." Sophie said. And I realized how very serious she was.

"I will talk to Theresia and come up with our plan, for you."

"It needs to be by two weeks, when I return. If I don't have it by then, you and your wife and boys are just left behind." Josip said.

That night when our quiet time came and Theresia and I were just starting to talk about our plans, we were interrupted by more bad news. Anna, Magdalena's sister, came pounding on the house's front door. She had ridden from her home in Zombor, eighteen kilometers away. Her eyes were black-and-blue. She was weeping. "It's terrible! Help me! Christian went crazy and was beating me. Father came up behind him and hit him in the head with something. Christian is dead! What am I going to do now?"

Konrad and Magdalena got out of bed and joined us in the sitting room.

After hearing what had happened Konrad asked, "Where is your father?"

"He packed a bag and left right away. I don't know where he went. He left our horse behind. For me, I think."

Konrad began questioning her. "Are you sure that Christian is dead?"

"Oh, my poor Christian! Yes, the blood and the brains, it was terrible. His eyes rolled back, his pulse stopped and his chest did not rise and fall. I sat on the floor for some time, holding his head in my lap. I had to change my dress and clean up before I left."

"Were the police summoned?"

"Not by me. Or anyone else that I know of."

"Who would come to your house next?" Konrad continued.

"I don't know. Police might be summoned by his work when he's not in for a few days. But with his drinking, who knows?"

"I think that you have some time. They will probably come here looking for you but we will check you into the Inn as a guest under a different name. Try to sleep now. Have a schnapps and try to calm down. It's all over now Anna and you will start a new and happier life. Magdalena will help you. Some of us will soon move from here, until the war is over. You'll go with them. Do you understand?"

"Yes Konrad, that's what I want to do."

"You'll need new identification papers, but I'll take care of that."

After everything had calmed down, Theresia and I tried to go back to discussing our future. But it was too much for one night. We put it off. There was still two weeks.

Konrad obtained new identification papers for Anna. When the police came looking for her, three weeks later, the papers held up. She was just a guest at the Inn. With her father's disappearance, they assumed that Anna was on-the-run with him.

The weather turned much colder. Christmas was approaching. Conversations about everyone's future, went back and forth in the house and around the dining room table for a few days. But the time was running short and tough decisions had to be made and passed to Josip. Theresia and I were still trying to decide.

We all sat down at the table on the final evening. I remember that the conversations went something like this.

Father Butscher said, "I shall stay! The Inn is my life and I will not leave it to be ruined. I will trust God to protect me from the heathens. Everyone else should go, but one way or the other your decisions will not change mine."

Mother Butscher simply said, "I stay with my husband to the end, if it comes to that. Period! The rest of our family should put their children first."

Whether their decisions were due to stubbornness or age, it did not matter. We all knew that there was no changing their minds.

Stephen spoke next. "I will stay with my parents. If the Inn needs to be defended from just a few Partisans, I can help with that better than anyone. As you all know, I have faced Serbians before. Konrad, what kind and number of weapons can you get for us?"

Konrad answered, "I'll have to see. But machine-guns for sure. I will stay with you and help defend if it's just a few. I would be drafted into the army anyway, if I tried to enter Germany. That would happen even with false papers. So, I might as well stay here and fight for my home. I'll try to continue doing business with Josip and, if possible, keep an emergency escape route open."

Magdalena was the hardest to convince. "I'll not leave Konrad. I can somehow help in a fight."

Konrad argued, "You must go, for the sake of Klein Mathias. He just celebrated his first birthday. You must put him first and give him the best chance for a good life. He could easily be killed here, or maybe worse grow-up under a Serbian government. They will not treat him well and I don't want anything like that for him. For his sake and for mine, please go while you have the chance."

Magdalena finally agreed, "Okay, okay, I see that our child comes first. I'll go."

Anna said, "I will go with Magdalena and help her with Klein Mathias."

Theresia was also hard to convince, and naturally didn't want to split up our family. But finally agreed after everyone else at the table urged her to take Adam. "I'll go with him because he's still too young to be drafted in Germany. And who knows what will happen here? If he stays in a frontline area some local commander could just sweep him up. Mathias has to stay with you, Johann, and hide out. If he tried to enter Germany, he'd be drafted for sure at his age. He will not take his last semester of school, and then maybe everyone will assume he was gone with me. But he has to stay in hiding."

Sophia first told us a secret, that she had been hiding. "Josip and I are engaged for the past three months. He asked me and I accepted and have stopped seeing any of the Inn's guests since then. I also need to stay in order to help Konrad with our business and maybe I can even make a deal to protect the Inn. So I'm staying."

In the end, two women and five men were staying and three women, a teenager and a toddler were going to Germany. Who could say which of these decisions would prove best? Our celebration of Christmas was muted by the impending departures.

We saw them off from the small dock along the Danube riverbank at the foot of the stairway from the Inn. They left by steamer right before New Year's Day 1944.

A chill wind was blowing that gray morning and almost everyone cried. Would we see each other ever again? They settled in the city of Ulm, Bavaria.

Then the newspapers reported on January 2nd that Hungary's First Army was mobilized to protect the northern Carpathian border of from the advancing Red Army. It was reported in the coming days that the fighting was going well for us.

Theresia wrote to me, "Ulm is a beautiful city and we are well received by its people. They ask many questions about conditions in our country and why we decided to leave. There are many differences in the local customs and dialect, but we all are adjusting well. We feel safe and lucky to be here, but we are all homesick. I miss you and Mathias very much. Please tell him that I love him and pray that he remains safe. Even though it has been only a couple of months, I'm beginning to question my decision to leave. What do you think? Should I change my mind and move back? The other ladies have similar feelings. It is lonely here, especially at night. And I even miss the bakery."

Then on March 19th, the newspaper headlines screamed *"Invasion by Germany"*. While Hitler entertained Horthy in Austria to discuss relations between our two countries, eight German divisions occupied us.

Hungarian forces had been given orders not to resist. There was nothing that we could do about it.

Soon the newspapers reported *"Horthy to remain head of state, but the Gestapo has arrested Prime Minister Miklós Kállay and other anti-German politicians. The new prime minister, Döme Sztójay, recommitted Hungary as Germany's ally, and cancelled Hungary's agreement with the Allies."* Soon after Allid bombers began attacking Hungarian targets.

Very soon the newspapers announced that all men between the ages of seventeen and forty-two were subject to being drafted and that they should report for duty. That would include Konrad, who was twenty-nine; Mathias, eighteen; and myself, thirty-eight. Only Father Butscher and Stefan would be left. None of us reported.

Within a month they came looking for us. Mathias was able to hide in the ditch by the river, until they left. As we had guessed, they assumed he was with his mother and brother in Bavaria, since no one had seen him at school this semester.

Konrad's father told him to hide in a laundry chute. A warning of the army's approach had just come in by way of one of Father Butscher's homing pigeons. They were not looking for Konrad here, since his last known address was outside of Futog, some eighty kilometers away.

But I was a different story. "Are you the baker, Johann Diplich?" the lieutenant asked. "We need your skills in the army. Nothing keeps up morale like good food." They knew that I owned the bakery, so I had to admit that it was me. They allowed me to pack a small bag of personal items before loading me on a truck. My basic training was only three weeks. The Sargent said, "We don't need you to march or shoot a gun. Just to make good meals for the troops."

I was assigned to Stefan's old unit the 7th SS Division Prinz Eugen. By May 25th, it was back in Serbia with an unsuccessful operation to kill or capture Josip Broz Tito, commander of the Partisan forces. Konrad wrote and assured me that Mathais was okay and was having some success taking over for me at running the bakery.

He also reported disturbing word-of-mouth from Budapest. All the Jews were forced into a ghetto.

From there, they are being deported by the train-load. No one knows how many, but a lot. No one knows their destination. Some are saying work-camps in Austria. A new officer, we had not heard of before, SS-Ostubaf Adolf Eichmann is in charge.

I said out-loud. "What is going on? They are all Hungarian citizens!"

It's September now, and I'm writing this from the hospital. I have full use of my mind and arms, but not my legs. The 7th SS was just in tough fighting against Bulgarian, Soviet and Serbian forces in the Nich Region. We had many casualties. A shell hit the kitchen tent and I was badly injured below the waist. Now gangrene has set in. There is not much that they can do for me except amputate a piece at a time to slow it down. I'm soon a goner, but wanted to get this story written while I still could. I believe that my suffering will soon end and that I'll see God in heaven. But it's important that people in the future know my story, I think.

Johann Diplich, the baker of Apatin

6

A SOLDIER'S TALE

Here I am in a work-camp, in what I'm told is Estonia. Time has run together for me. My name is Mathias Diplich. I'm one of a group of Hungarian soldiers, who surrendered to the Russians on February 13th, 1945. That was outside of Castle Hill, in Pest.

Many of us are still here, especially those with the SS tattoo of our blood type under our left arm. For all to see it there. We'll probably never be repatriated, even though the war has been over for years.

And now I'm flashing back on how the teachers, priests and nuns, treated me in school! Bastards! Even now as an adult, and in my present circumstances,

I have flashbacks and get angry at them. Beating me, as a boy, on the palms of my hands with a rubber strap. Who gave them the damn right? I wouldn't cry and tried not to flinch. I'd like to beat them now, with my fists.

Get it together, Mathias. Think about something else. Think about the war. Keep it fresh in your mind and maybe one day someone will ask you how it all happened for you.

The war between Germany and Russia broke out when I was fifteen. My family was Danube Swabians, living in Apatin on the Danube River. My grandparents owned the Inn there.

It went well for Germany at first, but then Stalingrad happened. Right after that, Hungary lost so many troops on the Don River, that everyone's mood changed. We wanted out of it, an armistice with Russia and the others. But Germany wouldn't have it and invaded us. Some of my family, including my mother and younger brother, Adam, had fled to Bavaria for safety from the Serbs. But I couldn't. At my age, I would have been drafted at the border. Turned out, that I was drafted anyway.

I was hiding in the ditch by the river. I had used it before, when they came in their trucks, searching for men of draft age. They had taken my father away. Even now, I don't know how he made out. My uncle, who was also eligible, was hiding in the Inn's laundry chute. His last known address was outside Futog, so they weren't looking for him in Apatin. But I was a different story. They had my school records.

First, they searched the house and found my stuff. I could hear my grandmother yelling at them. Then, they used their dogs to find me. Damn dogs! They just followed my footsteps. Came right to the ditch and barked. Onto the truck I went with the three others they had found that day.

Even the SS was drafting men. I was assigned to the 17th SS Volunteer Cavalry Regiment of the 22nd SS Cavalry Division, Maria Theresa. "Volunteer" was wrong, as there were no longer any of those, at least not in Hungary. We were sent for training to a nearby base located at Pesthidegkut, just northwest of Buda. It was September, 1944 and I had just turned eighteen.

All available units were being sent into the fight. Our Division's 52nd SS Volunteer Cavalry Regiment was shipped out to the eastern front to join the 9th Hungarian Division in its defense of Arad, Romania. We learned through scuttle-butt that it had not gone well for them. The Russians surrounded them and the few that survived had to swim the Mures River in order to escape.

My buddy, Alfred "Curley" Hess, and I saw some BMW motorcycles near our training field. We had just finished a long day of drilling and our feet were aching. I joked, "Curley, why march when we can ride?"

The more we thought about it, the better it seemed. So, we put in our papers and volunteered for reconnaissance. We were both transferred to the 22nd SS Panzer Reconnaissance Battalion, at the nearby Kisber facility. We loved riding those machines.

Around the middle of October, after only a little over a month's training, my battalion was activated. At Noon, we met up with four Tiger II tanks and a bunch of trucks carrying troops, including the 17th SS.

The Captain said, "Lead the way to the Regent's Palace. Here on the map. Follow this route through the city. And don't let anyone, including the police, stop you."

"With four tanks backing us up, that will be easy." was my first thought.

Six of us on motorcycles led the way, sweeping the route back and forth. We were familiar with the streets. The tanks were moving at a steady thirty kilometers an hour. The convoy, of about a hundred or more trucks and the rest of our motorcycles, was right behind the tanks. We did as we were ordered.

Going through the city center of Buda, you could tell from the way the civilians acted and the looks on their faces that they were afraid of us. I remember thinking "Why? Why afraid? We're here to protect them." At Regent Horthy's Palace, we were halted by a barricade erected at the entrance. Then we were ordered to surround the Palace and take cover.

"Curley, do you have any idea what the Hell is going on?" He shrugged. After a while, officers, under a white flag, approached the barricade. Heated negotiations went on for some time. At around 5:00 PM, the Hungarian units on the Palace grounds, began to fire at us.

"Hungarians shooting at Hungarians! That was really crazy." Curley shouted back, "They think we're Germans, Swabians in a German unit. That's it as far as they care." That really was like cold water in my face. All my life, my country was Hungary. Under orders, we returned their fire, but I made sure to aim high.

The firing only went on for about an hour and then petered

out. We held our positions all that night, taking turns at sleeping and sentry duty. At 8.15 AM the next day, we could tell that something was happening.

The barricade was opened and a number of large civilian cars entered the grounds. We saw Gestapo going inside the front door of the Palace. A short time later, the Regent and his wife were led out and taken away in one of those cars. We later learned that he had abdicated and was imprisoned in Bavaria.

The newspapers announced that Ferenc Szálasi took over the government. The regime's decrees were enforced by the brutal black-uniformed Arrow Cross Militia. Military personnel belonging to the Arrow Cross wore on the upper left sleeve an armband of red and white stripes with a white lozenge bearing a green arrow-cross. They were all real bastards.

While that was going on, the Russians were closing in on Budapest, trying to encircle it. My unit was back to the flatlands northwest of Buda. The Russians were already infiltrating the area.

We in reconnaissance would go out every day on our motorcycles and gather as much information as we could. It was dangerous work. We were shot at more than once, but my squad was lucky and nobody was hit.

One day when Curley and I were out patrolling, we were waved down by a woman. She asked, "Are you "Curley" Hess?"

"How do you know my name?" Curley asked.

"A little bird told us that you had a motorcycle that you would sell. Is that right?"

"It's a little tricky to do something like that."

"Just report that one of yours was shot-up at some other location, and that you had to abandon it. It will be easy money and you'll be saving two lives."

"What do you think, Matty?"

"Why not? It sounds easy." I agreed.

The woman went on, "Two men are coming to meet you right here and at this time of the morning, in four days. They will offer you a good price one of your motorcycles. You and your friend here will make some real nice money by selling them one of yours. But now that you've said yes, and everyone is counting on you, if you change your mind for any reason, they'll be caught. And you'll both have a target on your back. Understand?"

We made the connection and the sale. It turned out that these men were my uncles. I was so happy to see them, if even for a short time. And to help them get away. Not to mention that Curley and I had a wonderful time on our next leave with all that money.

In early November, the 22nd SS Cavalry Division was made part of the IX SS Mountain Corps, which was tasked with defending Budapest as a "fortress city", meaning until the last man. The weather became rotten and stopped us from riding. We began living in the trenches. "Curley, you have to be more careful and keep your head down. You'll get shot for sure." But they didn't get him until later.

I remember sitting in the trench and wishing that the girls we had been with on our leave were with us. But wishing wasn't going to change anything, would it? I had an MG42, the fastest machine gun in the war, and would fire it anytime we were attacked. I called it "my girlfriend". It and I must have killed some Russians, but you just don't know. You can't follow the bullets when you're getting attacked.

The weather improved a little and we were able to do some recon. The Russians had continued to infiltrate, and no one knew any longer where the front lines were. We reported back that it didn't look good. The officers decided that we had to fall back. On Christmas, the whole division was pulled back. Medals and decorations were awarded. I wasn't around long enough to get one. And my efforts were not all that different from any of the other men around me.

We marched all that night to Vecses southeast of Pest. We were defending the airfield. The next day Curley and I were ordered to set up our machine guns and guard a bunker, about fifty meters away, overlooking the road. We had two machine guns, mine that was good and Curley's an older one that was always jamming. Curley started monkeying with his to make sure that it would work.

Then Curley and I took turns going to breakfast. He went first and when he came back, I started to go. But right then an officer yelled, "Everyone out! The Russians are coming!" Then the bullets started flying like crazy. The Russians had broken through our front lines and the officers yelled for everyone to retreat.

Curley and I grabbed our guns and started to run. We found a good spot to set up and covered some other guys as they were falling back. Then he was hit and I knew that he was a goner. I started running and saw a Panzer II tank on the side of the road, stuck in a ditch. I kept running holding my machinegun. Russians were coming along the road maybe a couple-hundred meters away.

A truck sped down the road and a bunch of us waved it down. We all jumped on, but I dropped the machinegun as I climbed on. The Russians were throwing everything at us. Artillery shells were exploding all around, puffs of black smoke and debris flying everywhere. Soldiers on the road would get hit and fall. I saw the Panzer II tank get going behind us with some guys hanging onto the top. It rolled right over the bodies on the road.

I said to myself, "If I get through this alive, it will be a miracle and I'll start going to church."

All of a sudden, thirty meters behind us, there was red flame and black smoke. Shrapnel from the exploding shell tore into me, ripping off my left ear, and tearing into my left shoulder. I didn't even realize that I had been hit. I must have been in shock. Then, about thirty seconds later, the tank got hit and exploded.

The front of my white winter coat was all red, covered with the blood that was pouring down from my head. And I couldn't lift my left arm. The truck dropped me off at the first aide place and they bandaged me and put my arm in a sling.

At 7:00 PM that night I was put into another truck and taken to the main hospital at Castle Hill. A doctor saw me after midnight and sewed up the place my ear had been. Some of the shrapnel was removed but they couldn't get it all. They didn't have anesthetics or pain medications, so it hurt like hell, but I was lucky to be alive.

A week later, the first aide guy came to give me a new bandage. The blood had caked under bandage and into my whiskers on the left side of my face. He just grabbed the old bandage and pulled it away with no warning at all. Everything ripped away and the pain was unbelievable. My first reaction was to kill that son-of-a-bitch.

By the end of January, 1945, most of the troops had retreated into Castle Hill. Built in Buda, in the 13th Century, its four and five story high, with thick walls that could protect us from the Russian artillery and bombs. There are ports in those walls and machine guns fired out. The wounded were kept below in tunnels.

At first, I could walk and get around easily, so my job was to carry ammunition to the machine-gun positions. But during one of the Russian attacks, I slipped on the stone steps and went down hard. After that my knee hurt like crazy. I had to fashion a crutch out of some scrap lumber that was laying around.

As the Russians slowly surrounded and took Budapest, things got very bad in Castle Hill. There was hardly any food at all. If an animal, like a horse or a dog, was killed in the street by the shelling, soldiers would sneak out and cut a piece off. They tried air drops to us, but as much fell in the river or into Russian hands as reached us. It was winter and we were slowly starving.

By February 11th, everyone knew that the situation was hopeless. The officers told us that we could either try to breakout through German lines or we could surrender. On February 13th, I was among the five thousand or so who surrendered, many of us wounded. I learned later that, of the much larger number who tried to breakout, very few made it. Many thousands were killed by the Russians, in and around Budapest.

Some of us, who were judged strong enough, were culled out

to become slave laborers for the Russians. I was back to walking without the crutch, so I was put with them. Other prisoners who were wounded but could walk with crutches or a cane were forced to leave. They were told that they could try to walk home. Those too sick or wounded to walk were left down in the lower tunnels beneath the Castle. They had only lice infected beds of straw to sleep on.

I remember what I heard about those two thousand wounded men in the tunnels. Another soldier told me. The lice in their straw-beds were so bad that the Russian soldiers gave them gasoline to rub on their bodies to kill the lice. An explosion occurred and they were all burned up when fire tore through those catacombs.

On the first day as prisoners, we were forced to walk about twelve kilometers. On the second day, we walked until Noon to a kind of picnic area where all these Jews were gathered. The Russians told us about the ghetto that had been established in Budapest and about the death camps. They made us look at the Jews. I was naturally sorry for what they had gone through, but didn't feel that I had anything to do with it.

My knee was acting up again from all the walking, but I could still get along fairly well. They put us into a line, based on how healthy we looked. Behind me were six or seven other guys, limping worse than me. They were keeping up as best they could. One guy passed me, but others from in front of me fell back behind me.

After a while I heard a shot. I turned and saw that a guard had killed the last guy in line because he couldn't keep up. Then I saw him shoot the next slowest guy. We all walked as fast as I could. As the day went on, the pain in my knee was really bad, but I could shuffle along pretty well. I moved up in the line and passed some guys. There were more shots as the day went on. More guys that couldn't keep up.

The next day we were ordered to strip off our clothes. Then we had all the hair on our bodies shaved off. Our clothes were put into a very hot room. The buttons burned when we got them back but the lice were gone. After that, we were loaded into American Studebaker trucks and taken to a camp in Romania.

We were there about two months, and many people died in that hell-hole. For some reason, the Russians had quotas to fill and had grabbed civilians from the streets of Budapest. They took young and old. They took people raised on farms or in cities. I think that they must have over-estimated the number of military prisoners they would get from the battle.

I was still young and tough. But many people were just not tough enough to make it. The conditions were unbelievable. There were four-hundred in a space no bigger than my living room in Apatin. We had to lie down in rows with our knees bent, all facing in the same direction. To turn over the whole row had to turn. If someone died, they brought in a new guy so that there was always four-hundred.

For food, there was a weak cabbage soup at 2 AM and a cube of bread at 11 AM. Nothing more. It wasn't enough to live on. Weak ones died each day. A horse-drawn wagon came by once a day and we would drag the dead outside to be picked up. Sometimes a hundred a day died in the camp and their bodies were burned.

After those two months, we were loaded into railcars. I thought it was bad up till then, but this five-day trip was the worst. No food, no water, no nothing. Sixty or seventy men in each car lying on four vertical layers of wooden board platforms. Guys above, below and to each side of you.

When we got to our final destination in Estonia, life finally settled into a routine of work, and then more work the next day. Time ran together. But compared to all the things that had happened to us before, things weren't as bad. The work was hard, but at least there was enough to eat.

7

FLIGHT

It was the Fall of 1944 and the war was just over the horizon. But business was booming at the Inn, especially the tavern. No one wanted the party to end. Then they would have to face the reality of what was coming.

Stefan asked me, "What do you think? You and I need to decide when to go."

"It feels like a noose is tightening around my neck. There's little time left." was my response.

Partisan forces were moving north into the vacuum created when German and Hungarian forces were reassigned to either the Eastern or Italian Fronts. Bacs-Bodrog was a sideshow compared to the importance of Budapest or of Italy's Po River Valley. But, it was not a sideshow for the Partisans.

My main source of business had dried-up. The Partisans were getting, free from the Soviets, all the machine guns that they needed. I was helping mother run the Inn. Stefan was helping father run the tavern. Sophie was working there but had given up her private business, after getting engaged. But she was keeping her ears open for any information regarding prospects for Apatin and the Inn.

In mid-October, Josip visited. He told us, "It's time for you all to get out. In about a week the Partisans and Soviets will be here in Apatin. Any delay even now, and I'm not sure that I can help you leave. The Soviets are closing in on the Danube all the way up to Baja. You and Stefan are very vulnerable. I'll marry Sophie, if she'll have me, and that should protect her. But she will have to completely accept and support Serbia in order to be safe. That might even involve her turning someone in as a traitor."

"And what will Sophie's new last name be? You never did tell us your full name."

"My name is Josip Stambolic. So, your aunt's name will be Sophia Stambolic."

Stefan and I tried again to convince our parents to leave with us. We said to them, "You know that this is all about to end. Why don't you face that fact and move to Budapest? We'd all be safer there." But we had might as well be talking to the wall.

Our parents gave us that look. Father said, "You and Stefan go ahead, son. Mother and I have talked about it and we'll ride things out here. The fighting will pass us by and then it will just be the same as a few years ago, when we were inside Serbia's boundaries. We will just adjust our menu and the style of music that we play."

"No, father, it won't go like that. There will be repercussions and revenge against the Hungarians and especially the Swabians." But it was hopeless. They would not listen. If the Inn was on fire, Father and Mother Butscher would still not leave.

I was there when Sophie gave all of her foreign currency to Stefan. "Josip told me that if I'm caught with any of this, they would probably kill me. You use it to escape and to help the family in Germany. If we ever see each other again, you can give me back what you didn't need. Helping you will make me happy, so don't say no to me."

The next day Josip told Stefan and me, "I've arranged for a boat to pick you up at the dock at nine o'clock tonight. It will drop you off northwest of Buda. A car will meet you there and take you to near Kisber, where the 22nd SS Panzer Reconnaissance Battalion is stationed. That's your nephew Mathias' unit. He and his buddy Curley Hess will meet you, where the car drops you. Hide until you see them on their motorcycles. They'll sell you one and report it lost in action. There are Russians all over the place up there, closing in even now on Budapest. Mathias and Curley get shot at all the time. Head north as far and as fast as that BMW will take you."

"Wait a minute. What about Budapest! I figure that it will be the safest."

"You're wrong there, Konrad. It would be the worst place to go. I guarantee you that the Soviets will surround it and then do a number on it. Everyone will starve this winter. Once it surrenders, civilians will be picked up as prisoners-of-war. That's what's happening now in Romania to Hungarians with German sounding names. They are accused of being partisans. There are no trials for them. They are just deported to the Soviet Union, as slave-labor. If I were you, Konrad, I'd head for Slovakia."

Later, as we walked down to the dock at the appointed time, I noticed that Stefan was limping and had pain on his face.

"Stefan, why are you limping? Will you be okay to travel?"

"It's better to travel, than if I don't. Right? Staying is out of the cards. It would get me killed."

"What's wrong?"

"This false leg doesn't fit me very well any longer. There's a lot of irritation and now infection where it connects to me. I was warned about that but didn't want to use crutches. Now when I really need to travel, it's causing a problem. It's infected pretty bad."

"Can You ride a motorcycle?"

"Yes, I'll make sure not to slow us down."

The blacked out night-time trip up the Danube was nerve-wracking. The boat rode dangerously low in the water. It was obviously at its full capacity. The Moon had already set, which was a big help.

We could hear the sound of tanks and trucks moving around on the eastern shore. That must have covered the sound of our engine. In more than one place the boat seemed to pass right past the muzzles of the Russian guns. Fortunately for us, those guns were silent. Once past Baja it was better, and we docked in Pest at dinner time of the first day.

There we sat for the entire second day and into the next morning. Then the black-uniformed Arrow Cross Militia came on board. They all wore their red and white armbands, with a green arrow-cross. We had heard about them, even in Apatin. Their obsession with Nazism and the "Final Solution" made them feared by any non-Arian. They were searching for Jews.

Stefan presented his credentials showing his past rank and *Order of the German Cross in Gold* award. The black uniformed Lieutenant was impressed and we were immediately granted his approval to continue our journey. Even the Walther that Stefan was wearing was not questioned.

They went through the entire boat. We heard them ask the captain what he was carrying.

"Copper ingots from the mine at Bor. The mine itself is already closed down and just the smelter is open. This is probably one of the last shipments out of there. The Serbians are closing in with the advance of the Red Army. It will soon be in their hands. Even the labor-details are now pulled out and being marched back to Hungary. You'll have lots of them on your hands if they get here through the Partisans' lands."

"If they do, we'll put them on the trains to Auschwitz. We've only just this summer emptied their ghetto here in Budapest. Lucky for you that we haven't found any on-board your riverboat. You are cleared to proceed."

We were dropped off near Gyor, and as directed spent the night in a small inn. The next morning a car was waiting for us. Other than checking our identities the driver did not speak. He took us toward Kisber, and finally slammed on his brakes. He told us to get out and follow our instructions. So, we hid in the bushes there. It seemed like forever, until we saw our riders coming down the road. We waved them down.

"Hello, Matty!" We were a complete surprise for him.

"Uncle Konrad! Uncle Stefan! How did you get here?"

"We are your buyers. Which is the most reliable machine? This needs to be quick, so that no one sees and puts two and two together. We don't want to see you caught."

Curley said, "Take this one and get out of here, now. Let's have the money."

So, with quick good-byes to Matty and Curley, we were gone that fast. Up the road to Komarom we went and there we crossed into Slovakia at Komarno. You would think that they could spell it the same on both sides of the river. Wouldn't you?

The border guards asked, "What is the purpose of your travel?"

Stefan replied, "Medical treatment at Bratislava for my leg. It's infected. Do you want to see it?" They looked at Stefan's credentials briefly and that was it. They never even asked for mine.

But our luck was running out. When we reached Bratislava, Stefan couldn't go on. The pain was too much. The infection needed treatment. When we went to the hospital, they admitted him immediately. He needed surgery and would be there for weeks.

"Here is the Walther, my medal and the money from Sophie. I don't know how you'll be able to get across the border with these notes, but do your best and give it a try. It's up to you now, to get the money to Magdalena, Theresia and the kids. The gun and the medal aren't important to me. So hock them or just dump them. Whatever you think best."

"I know that we'll see each other again and it will be a happy time." With that I left him in the doctors and nurses hands.

That left me on my own in a strange city, with my out-of-date papers, a wad of foreign money, a motorcycle stolen from the SS and a Walther that I wasn't allowed to be carrying.

"If I ditch the BMW, I'm walking. I can't convert the money without showing my papers. But my papers were last stamped in

Futog, over three years ago. The first question would be, 'Where have you been?' This is not good, but staying here is out of the question. I have to try and cross the border into Austria. From Vienna, I might be able to jump a freight train to Munich. Maybe."

I cruised the streets until I found a large church. It was a quiet time of the day and it was easy to break into the Poor-box. I took the small amount of local currency and replaced it with a $50- US bill. Although what I got wasn't a large sum, it would be adequate for my purposes. Then I went to a local general store, and purchased some items.

My purchases included a sewing needle and thread, small pointed scissor, paper glue, cheese-cloth and the daily newspaper. Finding an inn that rented rooms by the hour, I went to work on my plan.

The larger Pound and Dollar notes were glued onto strips of the cheese-cloth, and then strips of newspaper over that. Carefully opening the stitching on lining of my coat I hung the strips all around the inside of the it with just one stitch each to hold them in place. Then those were hidden in the seam of the lining, as I sewed it all back together.

Around the inside of the should-pads, by the collar bone, I sewed in four bullets.

After cleaning up from my travels, I took time to eat a decent meal using the remaining smaller Pound notes. The inn's non-descript restaurant was cosmopolitan enough to accept foreign currency, although my Pounds did raise a few eyebrows. Leaving the BMW parked there on the street, I walked to the border-crossing a few blocks away.

"Purpose of your visit to Austria?" The border-guard seemed bored.

"Maybe I'll be lucky", I thought. "On my way to Ulm, by way of Vienna and Munich, to visit relatives."

"Any contraband or weapons?"

"Just my brothers sidearm, which I promised to look after for him and bring to the family home in Ulm. His leg is infected from a wound he received fighting in Serbia with the 22nd SS Cavalry Division. He couldn't travel any further. Now he is here in the hospital, for weeks it looks like. A hero, you know. Won the *Order of the German Cross in Gold* award. Asked me to bring that to Ulm too, for safekeeping with the family, until he gets out of the hospital. Want to see it?"

"Yes, that would be interesting. An honor just to look at it. A lot more interesting than all the other crap, that I have to look at all day."

So, I showed the medal to him, in its case. He was impressed.

"I can let you through with the gun, but it has to be unloaded. Let me have all of the ammunition you're carrying."

I unloaded the gun and gave him the ammo. But not the four rounds sewn into my coat. He passed me through without any further inspection. I thought it would be easy then to hitch a ride to Vienna. Finding some shrubs by the side of the road, I reloaded the Walther with the four bullets. That was a mistake.

As I stood by the roadside with my thumb in the air, the local Border Guard drove up. Two of them jumped out of their car and ordered, "Hands in the air." They searched me and found the loaded Walther. Since it was loaded, my explanations didn't do any good. The result was a six-month term in the local jail, two months for the gun and a month for each bullet.

The jail wasn't all that tough. All of the really bad criminals were either in the main prison, or sent to the Russian Front. They even let me keep my coat! And they let me keep Stefan's medal.

What turned out to be unlucky though, was my release date, which was May 5th, 1945. By that date, Hitler had committed suicide the week before and Germany was on the verge of surrender. And the Soviets were setting up their puppet government in Austria. Karl Renner was head of state. The NKVD was making civilian arrests. And as soon as I was released and walked out of the jail, I was picked up by them.

I was driven to their newly established headquarters in Vienna. A squat four story structure that had somehow survived the fighting. They put me in a small room with no windows. It had just the door from the hallway and a large mirror attached to another wall. It had a small table and two chairs, one on either side. They were bolted to the floor. The lighting was dim.

There I sat for three hours until two of them, a man and a woman, came in and grilled me. Without introduction or anything else, the woman said, "Your papers are false. No one ever went over three years under the Germans without their papers being stamped at least once. Who are you spying for? The Americans? The British? The Nazis? Tell us now if you know what's good for you! We have ways of getting the right answers from you, if you want us to do it the hard way."

"I'm no spy. I didn't want to fight for the Nazis, so I hid at my parents' inn in Apatin. Sold machine guns to the Partisans and laundered some money for them. You can ask Josip Stambolic."

"You had better be telling us the truth. He is a well-recognized name in our circles. It's even surprising to me that you know his last name."

"My aunt Sophie is married to him. I couldn't attend the wedding but I know that they were planning to tie-the-knit. They will know who I am."

They left the room and I sat there for another hour until I was escorted to a cell. The NKVD was efficient and it only took them three days. Then everything changed. They brought me cigarettes and coffee. They returned my coat. Nothing was said about anything in the lining. And the money was still there.

"The USSR will occupy the Eastern Sector of Germany. We need our man there in their Finance Ministry. Josip is well respected by us, and gave you a good recommendation. Says that you're very reliable. That you always do what you say that you will. He thinks you are a master of numbers. Can do stuff in your head. Is that true? It better be, if we pick you as our man."

"He talking about when I was changing money into different currencies for any number of people. I could just do it. Like that—I snapped my fingers—the right amounts came to me. I won't disappoint you on stuff like that."

Soon I was escorted from Vienna to Berlin by NKVD bodyguards. We rode in a private railway car. "What will your requirements be in Berlin?" the same woman asked. It was obvious that she had been assigned to me 24 hours, every day. When I slept, she must have slept but I could never catch her with her eyes closed. It became a game for me over the weeks ahead.

"First, I'd like to contact my wife, Magdalena. She lives in Ulm with my son Mathias. He'd be three now. I need to know if they're okay. And I want them to know that I'm okay. And where I'm going. We haven't heard from each other in close to a year. I want to invite her and Klein Matty to join me in Berlin, if that is allowed. It would be a great weight off my shoulders to have them with me.

Then, I'd also like to find out about my parents in Apatin, they own the inn there. And my sister Theresia Diplich and her son Adam, who were living with Magdalena. And Anna Theer who is Magdalena's sister and was also living there. Then there is my brother, Stefan who was in the military hospital at Bratislava when I last saw him some nine months ago. So many people to catch up on. And I can't forget, I want to hear from my Aunt Sophie and Josip Stambolic. Are they still living in Apatin? And Mathias Diplich. Last year when I saw him, he was with the 22nd SS Cavalry Division. How did they fare in the fighting? Did he make it?

It would be a great weight off my mind. That would help me to not be distracted in my new job. It's important to me that I find out about my relatives. Even if some of it is bad news, then I could deal with it, and move on. Please get me this information. I know that you can."

"And what about Ludwig Genser? You haven't asked about him."

"He is still alive!? We had given up hope. Yes I want to know about him. Does Aunt Sophie know? She should know as soon as possible."

"If we wanted Sophia Stambolic to know, we would have told her already. That information is for you only. Just you can do a lot for your family, Konrad Butscher, over the coming years. Do you understand?"

8

THE CASTLE

"Theresia, wake up. I had a bad dream about Konrad. Something's wrong. I have to try and find him before anything happens."

"Try to go back to sleep Maggie. It's the middle of the night."

"I'm so worried. I just can't lay here and do nothing. If I go, will you take care of Klein Matty for me? It could be a long time until I'm back. Who knows? Aunt Sophie's letter said that Konrad was headed here, but that was a month ago. The trip shouldn't take this long, unless he's caught up somehow in the war."

"Of course, I will, Maggie! As long as it takes. I'll watch over him like a hawk. You know how much I love him, even though his 'terrible twos' have started early. Now he's just like his mother."

"Oh stop you goof! Thank you so much! I don't know what I'd do without you. I'm taking the train to Vienna. It's still safe. I'll try and get down the river to Budapest, even if I have to float all the way. The river won't be frozen yet."

"But Maggie, the fighting around Budapest has already started. Isn't the city under siege with no way in or out? Maybe if you write to Aunt Sophie's new husband,

Josip. Maybe he could find something out about Konrad. They were always close."

"I don't know, but I have to find him!"

"You'll miss him when he comes here. Oh, please don't go! Even if you get into the city, how will you find him? If he's even there. You don't know. And it's so dangerous. You'll get killed or something worse. I've heard about the enemy's soldiers. No, I won't let you go and that's it!"

"You're right, I know. It's too late. I just have to wait. I'm not so good at that, but it's time to grow up."

"Maggie, let's talk about something different. I got that job I told you about. The one at the castle up in Hirschberg. They need women who speak Hungarian fluently. Regent Horthy was exiled there, after he was forced to abdicate. He wants to speak Hungarian to his staff and not German. You should try for a job there too. It will help keep Konrad off your mind."

"But who would watch Klein Matty? He's such a handful. He's into everything now."

"That's the best part, we could live at the castle. Actually, they want us to live there. There are lots of empty rooms and we could work out our schedules to always have one of us with him. I know that it can all be worked out, because they're asking everyone to look for Hungarian speaking women. Your sister Anna wants to try too. That will make three of us. It will be fun, to all do it together."

"And what about Adam? He's eighteen now and has to stay out of sight a little longer, until this damned war is over."

"He's coming with me. He's been hired as a translator for the Germans. They had to agree because very few of them understand Hungarian and the Regent refuses to speak in German. Adam was the only man they could find and we told them that he lost his papers and was sixteen and nine months."

"I can work just until Konrad gets home. That's all. Understood, okay?"

By Christmas, they were living and working at Hirschberg Castle. The women were on the domestic staff of Regent-in-exile Miklós Horthy de Nagybánya and his wife, Magdolna Purgly De Juszashley. She had often said to her friends, "We came to power in a decent way, through the door, but I fear that we will only get out of here, through the window." Now that they were under house arrest, it seemed that her fears were coming true.

Klein Matty turned out to be a favorite of the Regent and could do no wrong. He was spoiled that Christmas with lots of candy and toys from his new "Ompa".

Klein Matty often sat on the floor and played in the Regent's office. More than once, some new staff member came in to get the boy out of the way, but was told, "Just leave him where he is. He's fine right there. He likes to play near me."

He told Maggie, "Our own grandson, Istvan Junior, is only about a year older, but he can't be with us here. His father was killed fighting the Russians, when his plane crashed. My other son, Miklos Jr., was kidnapped, by German paratroopers. He is being held, by the SS, in Dachau. Ambassador Veesenmayer told me that unless I recanted my armistice and abdicated, Miklos would be killed immediately. So, I had no choice, I was forced to resign."

In October, the Regent had declared an armistice and stopped the mass deportation of the Jews, ordering the police to use deadly force if the Germans attempted to resume them. Then he sent his son to finalize the surrender terms with the Soviets. But the paratroopers forced their way into the meeting, trussed Miklos Jr. up in a carpet and took him to the airport.

The German Ambassador, Edmund Veesenmayer, took the Regent into custody at Castle Hill, and held him overnight. After the abdication, he and his wife were escorted here to the Castle as "guests of honor", and allowed to live in comfort. But, he is closely guarded by the SS. Maggie, Theresia, Anna and Adam continued to pray for Konrad and his safe return. And now also the same for Miklos. Even the Regent could not get any information about Konrad, who was overdue by at least 6 weeks. At Christmas, his prison held a modest celebration and a priest came in for a few hours and said Mass.

The holidays in Budapest were grim. The Russians had just succeeded in encircling the city. It was now cut off from resupply. Heavy shelling began on December 27th. Soldiers and civilians were starving by the time the last troops in Castle Hill surrendered on February 11th.

While Budapest was under siege, the Arrow Cross continued to hunt for Jews remaining in the city. Any they found were executed on the spot. Ferenc Szalasi, the, German installed, Premier of Hungary, fled Budapest. First, on December 9th, he went into the hills of Buds, then in March to Vienna and later to Munich. Senior members of the Arrow Cross joined him on all these retreats.

In early 1945 the Russians began "degermanization". Hungarians with German names, whether military or civilian, were deported to labor camps in the Soviet Union. In the first wave, a hundred thousand were rounded up from the streets of Budapest. Then there were more, in north-western Hungary, following the path of the advancing Red Army. In total, there were six-hundred thousand, not including the many who died in transit.

On April 16th, the U. S. Seventh Army advanced south on Nuremberg. The Germans put up a stubborn defense, including the use of anti-aircraft guns as ground weapons. In house-to-house fighting the city fell on the 20th. After that the Americans moved south toward Munich with little resistance.

The German guards at Hirschberg Castle fled as lead elements of the Twelfth Armored Division reached the Castle on April 29th. A Company of U. S. Military Police occupied the barracks that the Germans abandoned.

One of those MPs was Master Sgt. Paul Theer. Six months ago, he was ordered to report to Governor's Island, New York for reassignment.

"Thanks for dropping by today, Sargent Theer. I'm Mister Green. Sit down and relax. Call me Tom. I've been looking at your record and wanted to see if you'd be interested in something that's come up. We're forming a new volunteer unit that will be stationed in Germany. We need Hungarian speaking soldiers in it."

Wha'ya mean? Wouldn't you need German speaking men?"

"You would think so wouldn't you. But no, we're preparing for issues that will come up after the war ends. And one of the skills required for this particular team is to be able to speak Hungarian."

"What would it be doing?"

"We'll talk about that, but first let's go over a few things. Your file says that your parents were Swabian immigrants to America in 1907."

"Yeah, right. Around that year. I'm pretty sure."

"Did they speak Hungarian at home?"

"Yeah, and German. I picked both up from when I was a kid."

"Did they have any political leanings?"

"You mean, were they Nazis? No, they hated them. When I was first assigned to the MPs, my unit was escorting German POWs from the East coast to prison camps in the Far-West, California and all. Some of those guys were recalcitrant Nazis, and one of them spat at me. So, I responded by braking his jaw. When I told my folks that story, even Ma laughed out loud. I'm sure that Pa bragged about me to his buddies."

"yes, there is a note in your file about an incident with one of the prisoners. I was going to ask you about it."

"you guys do a pretty through job of researching people for your team. I don't know if I'm annoyed or impressed."

"Don't be annoyed, please! This is important for us to know before talking to you about what this unit will be doing."

"Okay, I'll keep listening."

"Good, I'm glad that you aren't upset. How about your friend dying that first day on the beach at Normandy? Does that still upset you?"

Paul stares at Mr. Green. It had been less than five months since his friend, Al Myers, a cop from the 25th prescient in New York City, had been blown to pieces by a German shell, right after reaching the beach on D-Day.

"I think about him a lot. I should have been right there with him.

Maybe it would have been different. Maybe we would have gone in a different direction. But I was in the General Army Hospital with appendicitis. We had been together all the way through basic and our training in England. We were getting ready to embark for France. It's just so strange. I haven't been able to figure it out. Why him and not me?"

"We're soldiers and just have to move on from stuff like that. Not let it get to us. Put it behind us. I've lost some friends too."

"Yeah, right. Mind if I smoke? I could hold off, if you want"

"No. Please, go ahead, Paul. The smoke doesn't bother me."

"Just like a lot of things."

"Well anyway, this unit will be guarding the ex-Regent of Hungary. The Germans just forced him to abdicate and are now holding him in a Castle in Bavaria. He has lots of enemies. Once we get there, we'll want to make sure that nothing happens to him. It's important that he stays alive. Especially until he can testify in front of the tribunals that will be set up to prosecute war criminals. Sound like anything that you'd be interested in?"

"Sure, why not. Better than hanging around New York, and eating up my parents' food rations."

"You'll be sent for additional advanced training in hand-to-hand, small arms, explosives, communications and counter-surveillance. And in your spare time you'll brush up on your Hungarian. Tell your parents that you'll be out-of-touch for a year, but nothing else. I'll be in touch and tell you when and where to report. Okay?"

"Got it."

Paul was at home in Queens, when his orders were delivered by courier. "Strange," he thought. He reported to the local armory at the time instructed.

A staff car arrived and he was driven to Fort Dix and ordered to a secured area. Other men were there and more arriving every hour. Eventually, he thought, "There are about two-hundred of us now." There was little of the usual chatter. Soon, ten trucks pulled in. The men were loaded up and driven, about two hours to a base that he didn't even know existed. There he excelled at his training and was promoted from Staff to Master Sargent.

On April 20th, they were loaded onto four stripped down B-29s and flown across the Atlantic to Scotland. After being fed and given a few hours to refresh, they were loaded onto three transport planes and flown to Nuremberg. They caught up with the Twelfth Armored just to the south of that city on the 23rd.

The Castle was liberated on the 29th. The next day Paul thought, "I might as well familiarize myself with this place." Most of the day-to-day operations of the company were left up to him. On his way through the castle, one of the first things he noticed was Anna Roth, Magdalena's sister.

"Good morning, I'm Master Sargent Paul Theer. I'm now in charge of security at the castle. What's your name, and what do you do for the Regent."

"My name is Anna Roth. I'm on the domestic staff. We clean and cook and do all the other things required to run the Regent's household."

Paul felt sure that if he didn't act now that the opportunity might never come again. "I apologize for being so forward, but I'd like to see you socially."

"That was forbidden with the SS soldiers that just left here. Isn't it also forbidden by your army?"

"Yes, it's forbidden, but I don't care."

She said, "When can we meet?"

Sometime months later, she would tell him, "When I heard your name, it seemed such a strange coincidence. My first husband, who is dead, his name was Theer. And while I was so attracted to you, my tall blonde American soldier, I couldn't help but think, *"Am I destined to always be a Theer?"* But then I thought, *"Your life is now going to take a new direction!"* And so, I agreed to meet you."

On May 1ˢᵗ, the American MPs arrested Regent-in-exile Miklós Horthy. Mr. Green arrived minutes afterwards. Master Sgt. Theer said, "The bastard is in his office. I have three men watching him."

"Good. Show me the way."

"Regent Horthy, my name is Thomas Green. I'm with the American government and it has given me the responsibility for your safety. Our purpose is to get your testimony at some of the trials that will be held for war criminals. Until then we will be moving from location to location. Master Sargent Theer's MPs are well trained and will see to it that you are safe. Do, without hesitation, as they instruct. You have many enemies who would like to see you dead. The MPs have established safe-houses. You'll be moving from one to the next. Now get packed and ready to go. Pack light. We can replace things but we can't replace you."

"In my youth, I have seen action with the Austrian Navy. I led Hungary all these years during depression and war. I've stood up to Hitler and the Arrow Cross. I'm not fearful now in my old age. I will cooperate fully. I want the opportunity to testify."

Later Mr. Green told Paul, "After the last war, his country begged him to become Regent. He spent the next quarter-century steering Hungary between the two giants; Germany and Russia. He made mistakes, but we feel that his decisions were predicated on keeping Hungary independent and avoiding invasion by one or the other of the giants. He had to make many compromises and in other cases just a stood by, when resistance was demanded. Now within the past year both armies invaded his country and what have his equivocations accomplished? Nothing. But he has tried to do some good things and I actually feel sorry for him."

"All I know is that he helped the Nazis kill a lot of Jews. And that I have a lot of friends who are Jews."

Paul and Anna had one chance to be lovers before he had to leave. But it was enough. Paul told her that they would be together as soon as his mission was over. Then they would spend the rest of their lives together. They both believed that. And soon Anna learned that she would have the child that she always dreamed of.

On May 17th, two weeks after Mr. Green, Paul and all the other MPs went off with Regent Horthy, a stranger knocked on the front door. "I'm searching for Magdalena Butscher." He said. Then after she came to the door, "I am a representative of the Soviet Union. We were looking for you in Ulm." Maggie's knees began to shake and she could barely stay standing.

"Your husband Konrad is well and sends his greetings.

He would like for you and Klein Mathias to join him in Berlin. He now holds a key position with the KDP, the Kommunistische Partei Deutschlands, which is helping establish the new government in the Soviet occupation zone. I am at your disposal to take you to him."

"He's alive! Konrad's alive! Oh, thank you God!"

Anna and Theresa chimed in, "Oh thank you, thank you God!" They all hugged and cried.

"I can be ready to go in an hour. But Klein Matty, I don't know. I'm not sure that I want to take him there. What are the conditions like in Berlin? The reports that we've heard are that the city is now just rubble."

"Most of it is pretty bad, but we are in a district that was spared from the bombing and the worst of the ground fighting."

"Why is that?"

"Because the KDP was in touch with the Soviet military. And most of its members live there. I strongly encourage you to bring him. Konrad misses him and especially wants to see him. He can be distracted from what he's doing. And you should thank the Soviet Union too for Konrad's safety."

Theresa spoke from behind her. "I told you, that you can leave Matty with me. Remember when we talked a few months ago? You must go, but he should stay with me."

"Oh, thank you. You're so sweet!"

"This is a mistake. Konrad will be disappointed. He misses his son. Won't you bring the boy this once? Theresa can come with us, and then bring him back here if you find that it isn't suitable for him."

"Then it's settled. The three of us will go."

The man reached into his pocket and pulled out a medal which he disgustedly threw on the table. "Konrad said that this is Stefan's. He does not want it with him in Berlin. Konrad said that he left Stefan in the military hospital at Bratislava last October. And that his brother's wish was that this get back to the family. We have not been able to locate Stefan."

"My sister, Anna, can hold it for him. She is staying here along with Adam. I just hope that Stefan is well and makes it home to us."

They left for Berlin that day. Theresa returned to the Castle after a week. She shared the news that Ludwig Genser was alive, in a Russian work-camp. She wrote to her aunt immediately, but knew that her letter might never get delivered. Klein Matty stayed with his parents in Berlin.

Paul continued guarding Horthy as they moved between safe-houses over the next months. The MP company was divided into five, forty-man, platoons. One platoon, Paul's, remained with Horthy throughout.

Each of the other four would find a safe-house in a remote area, put in phone lines for direct communication with Seventh Army headquarters, build defensive positions and clear fields-of-fire. When Horthy arrived, there would then be eighty men defending him. When he left for the next safe-house, Paul's platoon plus thirty-five of the forty from the current safe-house would go with him. When they returned, the platoon would clear the site and find the next safe-house in their area.

This continued until September when Horthy was delivered to the prison facility at Nuremberg. He provided evidence to the

International Military Tribunal in preparation for the trial of Nazi leadership. American court-officials did not indict him for war crimes and he was released in December.

Mr. Green had Paul come to his office for a meeting. "Paul, I know that you are anxious to go on leave and get back to your girlfriend down at the Castle. But before you go, I want to discuss the future with you."

"Anna's letters told me that she is expecting our baby in late February. I want to marry her before it's born. And then get them both to New York, so that I can get my discharge and go back to being a civilian. That's my future and there's not much to discuss."

"It's more complicated than that. Your country needs you here. The Regent will be living in Weilheim. He still has enemies, the Arrow Cross, the Serbs and even some Jews. In the meanwhile, the Soviets are acting out and trying to bring more European countries under their sway. I'm with the Overseas Service of the US government and you are very well positioned to be our man in Barvaria."

"How so?"

"Well think on it, Anna's sister, Magdalena, is Konrad Butscher's wife. And he is high in the communist movement in Berlin. Theresa is Konrad's sister. Both are part of Horthy's household staff. And we hear that Stefan has been found by the Arrow Cross. They could be bringing him to Weilheim, as soon as the Regent moves there. The OSS can take care of your discharge and marriage, make sure that your baby has American citizenship by flying your wife there now for the birth; and give you a career serving your country."

9

THE BYSTANDER'S PRICE

It was the 24th of October, 1944. Konrad and Stefan, you left only two days before this story starts. It is meant for you and for Theresia—you our children. It is written by my hand, as you can see, and with the hope that you will eventually read it.

It was morning and I was on the Inn's roof. One of my carrier-pigeons circled, and landed. She entered the coop ringing the little bell and went to a perch. The pillbox on her leg meant that there was a message. Going into the coop, I picked up a few kernels of corn with my left hand, and tossed one on the floor. She fluttered down and lowered her head to pick it up. I grabbed her with my right hand.

The message read, "Large Partisan forces coming your direction." It was not unexpected, but it confirmed for me that everything was about to change. I just didn't realize by how much.

For centuries, armies of many nationalities had used the Danube River valley as an avenue of attack. And warning systems had been set up along the river to tell of their approach. Whether by horse, pigeon, smoke or semaphore the native peoples had passed along these warnings, up or down the river. Carrier pigeons were now in favor.

The radio reports said that the defense of eastern Hungary had collapsed. And now the Russians were extending their front-line over to the Danube in order to begin the encirclement of Budapest. Behind the Russians, the Partisans were moving north, out of the mountains, which had been their refuge.

German forces had retreated to the defense lines around Budapest, and Croatia, on the west side of the river. Apatin, on the east side of the river lay undefended. And for our little Inn, it was a good thing, as the fighting and shelling would pass us by, at least for then.

I went over to the house to break the news. Mother was in the kitchen, preparing the tavern's evening supper and desert dishes. It was always a pleasure of mine to watch your mother while she worked. As you know, we are married for thirty years, and owned the Inn for the last twenty.

I will now give you my conversations with everyone, as best that I remember them.

"Mother, I received a message, by one of my pigeons, that the Serbians will be here later today."

"God's will be done. He will protect us."

"I'll tell Josip. It will go better if he is out front to greet them. And he will protect us, being so high in rank with them."

"Yes, my new Serbian-Orthodox brother-in-law. What have you done, my sister Sophie? Did you need a new husband that bad?"

"You should have at least attended the wedding. She invited us."

"Our priest told me not to go. And you should not have gone either!"

"It was necessary on so many levels. And it was a nice wedding. They both looked very happy. Your sister is beautiful, even at her age."

"And me at my age?"

I had walked into that, and so, I didn't say another thing. I turned and went to find Josip.

"Josip, it looks like your army will be here later today." He was busy cleaning glassware and getting the tavern ready for tonight.

"How do you know that?"

"A little bird told me."

"What?"

"A message came in on one of my pigeons."

"Don't tell me anything else. Like who sent it. I don't want to know. And don't mention your birds to anyone. It will only go bad for you."

"I'll take your advice. Thank you."

"Nothing will happen, with regard to you or the tavern, until the military situation is resolved."

"What does that mean?"

"It means that we are Communists."

"Also, now in-laws, as you know."

"Just let it go at that, Mr. Butscher."

Later, around 1:00 PM, the Serbian column of vehicles pulled up. It consisted mostly of American Jeeps and Studebaker trucks. A general stepped from the second Jeep and looked around as though expecting someone.

Josip walked out from the tavern and extended his hand. They bear-hugged.

That evening Josip entertained a large group of officers and officials in the dining room and tavern.

They had appropriated all of the Inn's rooms without telling me. Along with Mother, Sophie and the rest of our staff, I helped serve them.

I overheard them speaking in Serbian about how, a month earlier, one of their units caught up with a column of Jewish prisoners being marched to Hungary, from the copper mine at Bor. The Swabian guards had mistreated these Jews at Bor and now, on this march. They were beating them mercilessly and shooting stragglers.

The story went, how the Partisan unit caught and disarmed the guards. Then the Swabian officers and most blood-thirsty soldiers were executed on the spot. More than a few of them by the woman who was now sitting in the tavern. Other guards, who were freed, mostly Bosnians, joined the Partisan ranks.

I didn't know what to think. Had the Swabians become blood-thirsty due to their experiences in this awful war? Were they being ordered to do such terrible things? Were they pushing the prison-ers hard because they were fearful of being caught by the Parti-sans? Was it German indoctrination?

Before the Nazis took over, we Swabians in Bacs-Bodrog had never mistreated Jews. They lived among us all the time, but always separate from us. They wanted it that way so as to practice their religion and remain kosher. We didn't think of them as part of our culture, rather always as the 'other'. To us, they just didn't register, in our day-to-day society.

The Jews were so different that we could never really commu-nicate. And Hungary's politicians had taken advantage of them in 1938 with laws that allowed anyone to bring complaints against one of them. That would get the Jew sent for 'labor-service'. Very unfair, but we were not part of Hungary until 1941. And then Swabians didn't have enough influence to change these laws.

Then we were invaded by Germany, when all we Hungarians wanted, after the Don River, was to get out of this war. The Arrow-Cross people took over and Eichmann and his bunch imposed the 'Final Solution'.

All those Jews forced into ghettos and then deported. Tell me, how we Swabians could have prevented it. And what was it supposed to get for us? It tied up all the transportation capacity and so it didn't help at all with our defense against the Partisans. Or, for that matter, the Russians. How stupid it all was!

It just felt like we were watching a flood or some other natural disaster. We were watchers, bystanders, that couldn't do anything to change what was happening. Or was it that we wouldn't do anything? And now, our sons were committing such atrocities!

Was that all because we had made a deal with the Devil? I had sleepless nights going over all this in my head.

One of the Serbians, the woman in the story that was the executioner, paid the bill in Serbian Dinars. Sophie told her, "These are worthless now. Don't you have anything else?"

The woman snarled at Sophie, "This is the currency of what is now your country. You will accept them!"

Then they left, leaving behind broken glassware, dishes and lamps. They put Josip in charge of the Inn and also advised him that he would be serving on the Central Committee that would meet in Belgrade. He quickly assured us that Mother and I would continue to run everything.

Even if they had paid with Hungarian Pengo" or Croatian Kroners, it wouldn't have mattered. Inflation ruled the land and those currencies were all just about worthless. They had no backing with gold reserves.

For most transactions, we were in a barter-economy, trading commodities and services to each other. That worked very well for us, as we had a large store of liquor, wine and beer, all of which were highly prized.

The battlefront was quiet for a few weeks. Everyone seemed to be regrouping and resupplying for a major battle. When it started on November 11th it was right on our doorstep. For a week, the fighting was all around us, but never in Apatin.

On the 15th of November, the Russians crossed the river just upstream from us and established a beachhead on the west bank. The fighting raged there for two days, right in our sight. But the Inn was never damaged.

Then the fighting moved north and lasted until the end of the month. We could hear it the whole time. The Germans were pushed back. That was the extent of it for us, but the encirclement of Budapest continued.

Then on the 21st of November the hammer fell. The newspapers and radios announced Tito's and his

President of the Yugoslav Parliament's (AVNOJ) decree:

"All Swabians are now considered collectively hostile to the

State and all of their property is subject to immediate confis-
cation. This law applies equally to all Germans; all citizens of
Yugoslavia who are of German nationality, regardless of their
citizenship; and all collaborators."

That put us in the same position as the Jews before us, in Germany and then Hungary. And it was terrifying! We did not know which way to turn.

Fortunate that we had Josip and Sophie to hide us and protect our interests. Surely this was a temporary thing that would be lifted at the end of the war. The war that Germany was rapidly losing. We could stay in hiding until things got better.

We passed Christmas and New Year's like that. Hiding out and praying to Christ for protection and for luck. Josip was called to his Committee in Belgrade. Sophie handled all the business matters.

On February 2nd, 1945, the newspapers announced that this decree now had the full force of law. Anyone disobeying it was putting themselves into unspecified jeopardy. By the next day, the newspapers highlighted the first trials and resulting executions for not obeying this law.

Josip returned home on the 5th. He reported, "I tried to talk them out of it, but it was what Tito wanted. The Committees are supposed to have authority in such matters but no one wanted to stick their neck out. You'll have to stay in hiding for now." That was not good news.

Mother and I were bored out of our heads, just sitting around all day and only getting to go outside late at night. We ventured out one day to take the sun on our patio. We were seen by the postman who recognized us.

Budapest surrendered to the Russians in mid-February.

In March, it got even worse. By carrier pigeon, we received word that the Serbians were doing extensive searches. Then, a message said that entire villages were being emptied of all Swabians. They were all being sent off to labor camps.

Josip told us, "I can still get you across to Croatia, and then through Slovenia and Austria, to Bavaria. You could find your family through the Red Cross. The war is almost over. It's not a guaranteed trip, but it can still be done."

"I'm not leaving my home." Mother said.

"You might come to regret your decision. Bad things are about to happen here. Please reconsider for everyone's sake. It's not too late, but it has to be now." He tried to reason with her. But to no avail.

Two days later, we were looking out a front window watching any activity on the street. A Jeep and two trucks pull up in front of the Inn. An officer got out. A squad of soldiers emerged from the first truck. We ran to our hiding spot in the laundry chute. Josip was not there. After a while they found us. They pulled us out and with bayonets to our back marched us outside.

Sophie yelled, "You can't do this. Josip Stambolic lives here. He will be home soon and tell you that you can't have these two people. They are old and not anyone's enemy. You have to wait until he gets home and tells you."

"We know who lives here, Swabian whore. If it was up to me, we'd take you too. Now get out of my way."

A truck took us and four others the thirty-five kilometers north to Gakovo. A labor camp, they called it, but in reality, it was a star-vation camp. Men and women were separated into overcrowded wooden barracks. Thank God winter was over as there was no insulation or heat. But it was still very cold at night.

We were all put to work in the fields as part of the collectiv-ization effort. Our camp had about five thousand workers. In the four years that I was imprisoned there, about a third of them died from malnutrition. My heart breaks to tell you that Mother was one that didn't make it. They were very cold about the way they told me and then burned her remains. Her ashes were used as fer-tilizer, but God will find her there in the end. I'm sure that He will.

So here it is in 1948. Now, July, I think. After they let us go, I walked the 35 Kilometers back to the Inn. No ride this time. It was tough with the heat.

I'm writing this from home. There are so many Serbians around here now, it is all different.

There is something important going on with Josip. I saw a newspaper dated June 28th, 1948. Stalin has issued something called the "Cominform Resolution". I'm not sure what you've heard but Tito is breaking relations with the Russians because of it.

Josip is somehow caught up in it. I think that he is one of those considered to be supporting the Russian side. Sophie is very concerned. I'll add a P.S. at the end, if anything comes of it.

If there is something that I've learned from all these experiences, it's that people want simple answers for how bad things happen. Even if the facts don't support a simple conclusion. I know now that that's the way it is. It is just human nature for people to want to simplify things in their minds.

Kill Hitler, punish the other Nazis, execute the Arrow Cross fanatics, hunt down Eichmann if they can ever catch him, execute all our soldiers who surrendered in Slovenia, expel the Swabians. Now it's all taken care of. No one else is to blame for anything. The rest is all good. But it isn't, and the others who committed atrocities, will escape punishment and most likely do it again.

If there are a series of gruesome murders in an area or town, they are inevitably lumped together to become the work of one monster. It's easier that way to grasp it. People are frightened by the complicated truth that part of human nature is evil and that there are many evil people around us.

If one monster is caught and eliminated then the people feel that problem is solved and everyone can rest easy. Most likely there are other monsters out there who have committed some of those same crimes. The hunt for real answers ends and those others go free to kill again.

The Swabians are all lumped together with the Germans and by extension, we are all just as guilty in their minds. But I know that I couldn't have done anything to stop the atrocities. I'm not guilty, but I've paid dearly for just being a bystander.

And nothing is solved except people brush their hands together and say "That takes care of that."

I do not know where any of the three of you are and when you will see this, but I just know that someday you will. God bless you all and your families. I hope to see you some day.

Your loving father,

Mathias Butscher

P.S.—I'm adding this at my first chance. We have stopped for the night. Sophie and I are now walking to West Germany. We hear that we can enter and stay there. I have terrible news. Josip has been executed. Tito has purged his party and the government of all those even suspected of being Russian sympathizers. Once Josip was accused, things all happened so fast. A car pulled up in front. Four men in uniforms got out. They came into the tavern and called, "Where is Josip Stambolic? We have orders for him!" Josip was there and said "I am he." They pulled out hand-guns and shot him right there, without another word. He ran out onto the patio, but they shot him again, in the back this time, and he died there. Sophie ran to his side and held him in her arms. Then they forced her down and cut off all of her hair, down to almost the skin. She was stripped to the waist and with guns on her and blows, forced to walk out of town with her hands behind her head. All the while the Serbians in town were taunting her and calling her bad names. I caught up with her as soon as I could and got her dressed. Now we are walking to a better place. Good-bye to our Inn.

I fear that I will never see it again.

10

WEILHEIM

The town's train station was destroyed by an air raid on 19 April 1945. And there were many other scars from the war, in this old Bavarian town.

The "Peace" was chaotic and violent. Days after Germany's surrender, terrible reprisals began against the ethnic German populations of Eastern Europe. Twelve million people would be displaced; three and a half million would lose their citizenship and be forced to migrate to Germany; three-quarters of a million were confined in squalled prison camps; and half a million ultimately die from these ethnic cleansings.

In Czechoslovakia and Poland self-appointed tribunals tried and sentenced to death thousands of Nazi officials, soldiers, police and collaborators; and their families. They employed public hangings, firing -squads and beatings-to-death. In some instances, there were hundreds of deaths at a time. Children, even the youngest, were not spared.

The civilized world acted as "bystanders" to all of these reprisals, which were taken against both guilty and innocent ethnic Germans. Eventually amnesties were granted for all "occurrences" before October 28th, 1945. And then these atrocities were forgotten by the outside world.

In December, ex-Regent Horthy was allowed to rejoin his family. Adam watched, from a ground-floor window, as Nikolaus von Horthy stepped out of the green sedan, and was immediately surrounded by his wife Magdolna, his son Miklos Jr., his son's two daughters, his widowed daughter-in-law Countess Ilona Hona E delsheim-Gyulai, and her son Istvan Jr., aged four. They hugged and kissed like any family would.

Adam paid particular attention to the two teenaged girls. He had gotten to know them during the months that they had been here, waiting with their father, for their grandfather's release. Nicolette was sweet and adventurous, but at sixteen, a little young for him. It was Zsofia, just a year his junior, who he had a real crush on.

He could hear the old man say in Hungarian, "I'm so happy to see all of you. All together at last! And I'm so happy to be finished with my testimony in time for Christmas! I missed you all so much!"

Adam knew that it was the first that Horthy had seen his son Miklos, Jr. in fourteen months. Miklos, Jr. had been kidnapped by German paratroopers and detained in the Dachau concentration camp. Then in April he and other prominent inmates were taken to Tyrol, Austria. There, they were all finally liberated by the American Fifth Army on May 5th.

Four days before that, the ex-Regent Horthy himself had been kidnapped, by American MPs. Adam heard Horthy go on to say, "So much to catch up on. I want to hear everything. I'm done, for now at least, with those intense lawyers. But, I'll most likely be called back to give testimony against that damned Ambassador Veesenmayer. For now, it's time to put all of that aside and to enjoy this time together. I wasn't certain that we would ever see one another again. I prayed so often for this day!"

They all went to Midnight Mass and Adam sat in the pew behind, as close to Zsofia as he could. Afterwards the family retired to their private quarters in their villa, near the Roman built "Via Raetia". The road that was built in 200 A.D., to go over the Alp's Brenner Pass.

Adam was left standing outside, with his mother, who gave

him a hug and wished him "Merry Christmas". It was nice, but it wasn't the hug that he wanted.

Horthy slept well and awoke to the usual Christmas morning, together at last with his family. There was a hearty breakfast and then the exchange of presents. In the early afternoon he and his son, who was his political advisor, met to begin planning what they would do next.

"Father, I've gotten to know the members of this family who are working on our staff. They all live here with us. For a simple family on the surface, what an extraordinary bunch they are! They have important connections all over Europe."

"How do you mean, son?"

"You haven't met Stefan yet. He is the mystery-man. As an officer with the Seventh SS, he lost a leg at Tjentiste. He received the 'Order of the German Cross in Gold', for his bravery there. He was delivered here the other day, by men that are known to be Arrow Cross. It's possible that he may have come under their influence, so we will have to watch what we say around him."

"A man with question marks on his profile. How fitting for around here. Who else is with us?"

"Paul Theer, who I think works for the American spy service. He has diplomatic immunity, but he's no diplomat. You know him. He was the Master Sargent in your MP detail. He arrived here in early October, and married Anna Roth, who is on your staff.

Anna is Magdalena's sister, you know, Klein Matty's mother. Anna is expecting Paul's baby after the first of the year. She left to have it in America, so that it would be a citizen there. She's expected to return soon after that, with the child.

Did you know that Anna's father killed her first husband and then went into hiding? So, he may be lurking out there, if he's still alive."

"Well that is quite a family. And where are Klein Matty and his mother?"

"I'm not finished, father. They are in Berlin with the husband, Konrad Butscher. He holds a high position in the finance ministry of the new government that the Soviets are forming for their zone in Germany. Magdalena and the child may stay there permanently. I know that you're fond of that little boy, but we'll have to wait and see what she does.

Konrad's sister, Theresa Diplich and her son, Adam Diplich, are also here, and on your staff. The young man is your interpreter for German. If you wish to continue speaking Hungarian."

"Yes son, I'm more comfortable in my native language, even though I'm fluent in German. But I'm fond of him. It won't hurt to keep him on the staff and I'll pretend that I need him. And from what I've gleaned in only a day, my granddaughters would be very upset with me, if I kicked him out. Where is his father?"

"He was lost in Serbia while with the Seventh SS. He was a baker by trade, and was wounded by artillery fire that hit their kitchen. He died from his wounds.

Adam's older brother, Mathias, may be in a Soviet work-camp. We know that he was with the Twenty-Second SS when they were defending Budapest. Or he may be among those that didn't make it out."

"It was the Twenty-Second SS that surrounded Castle Hill, when I was forced to surrender. And then the Germans kidnapped you, Miklos, and forced me to resign. I'm not overly fond of that unit, even though it's mostly Swabians."

"Well father, try to let bygones be bygones and remember that they were under orders from the Germans. I've heard stories that when ordered to fire they shot over our soldiers' heads, so that they wouldn't kill fellow Hungarians."

"How do you feel about the Swabians, son? Are they German or are they Hungarian? The three Allied powers have decreed that all German populations should be expelled from Poland, Czecho-slovakia and Hungary. So, what does that mean for them? There are so many people now who feel they are without a country. That just doesn't seem right. There are about half a million people of German heritage who were citizens of Hungary. And that includes a good number of Jews. But people want their revenge. That's all there is to it. The expulsions will start and the trains will be coming here. We Hungarians need to decide how to treat them."

"You're right we need to talk about that, but allow me to finish with the family run-down. You should also be aware of Konrad's and Stefan's and Theresia's aunt, Sophia Stambolic. Her husband Josip is on the Central Committee of Yugoslavia. He helped get arms and cash to the Partisans during the war and is a hero for them.

We understand that Konrad and Sophia were helping in his efforts and that he got Konrad and Stefan out of Apatin, when the Partisans were about to close in. But their father and the mother would not leave their inn and were then arrested in March."

"With such information sources, it's no wonder that the Americans want a spy here. Connections with Berlin, Belgrade, maybe the Arrow Cross and us, all under one roof. We will have to cultivate these sources ourselves."

"And what can you tell me about our situation here, father?"

"We are still very much under the protection of the Americans, and will remain that way for quite a while. Of all our enemies, the Yugoslavians and the Arrow Cross people are the most danger-ous. The risk with the Soviets is greatly reduced. Stalin told Tito to be more forgiving. Not to judge me so harshly, because I tried to get an armistice in 1944. So, it's likely that the Soviets aren't after me. But I would have loved to have seen the look on Tito's face. He may not be ready to give up. And the Arrow Cross is nearby and we can bet that they have not forgiven my efforts to save the remaining Jews, before I was forced out."

"You stopped the deportations to Auschwitz, and that saved many of the Jews in Budapest, from Eichmann and those Arrow Cross bastards. Some say, because of that, you saved more Jews than anyone else did during the War."

"Well, our risks are reduced, but they're still there. You can tell, because the Americans continue to guard me. Their MPs may have been cut back, from a Company to a Platoon, but they're still here. Meanwhile, we must do everything that we can to get Hungary away from the Communists. That will now be my main goal in life. And even with Stalin being willing to forgive me the war, he will not appreciate what I'm now trying to do."

Soon, the Soviets on the Allied Control Commission insisted that Hungary begin the expulsion of their German population. There was some resistance in the government, but the key consideration, it turned out, was to provide housing and economic opportunity for Hungarians who had fled from neighboring states back into Hungary. The trains began to roll in January, 1946. They would continue until June, 1948.

During April: Magdalena and Matty returned from Berlin; Anna and baby Elizabeth returned from New York City; the new East German government was officially formed and Konrad Butscher became a top technocrats of the Deutsche Wirtschafts-komission (DWK)—the German Economic Commission; and financial support for Horthy's household began coming in from U.S. Ambassador to Germany Herbert Pell and from Pope Pius XII, a personal friend of Horthy.

Stefan waited until he was alone with Theresia and Adam. He called for them to sit with him at the kitchen table. "The three of us need to talk in confidence. I can't include Magdalena and

Anna, for reasons that will be obvious once I express myself. May I do that, speak my mind, with the expectation that it won't get back to them?"

"Yes, of course. I'm your sister. Tell us what's such a secret. Adam will also respect your wishes."

"I don't want any secrets from either of you. I need to know where you stand on some things and you need to know my stance. The gist of it is that we have to commit to the idea that we are now Germans and not Hungarians. They have rejected us, not the other way around. And Germany has accepted us. I've made that adjustment in my mind and want the two of you with me on it. Germany first!"

"I know what you mean, Uncle Stefan. That's the right way to think. This is my home now. I will be here the rest of my life, and loyal to this country. I have to strive to make Germany a success. And not care about a place that has kicked us out the door."

Theresia said, "I agree. I make that commitment too, my brother."

"Our problem then is that everyone else in this villa has a different loyalty. Anna will live in the United States as soon as her husband is transferred back home. We can't be sure about Maggie and our brother, Konrad. Do you think he's a captive there in Berlin? He has such a high position with the Communists, but who knows? And Horthy and his whole family are obviously still loyal to Hungary. They will put our old country above German interests any time. And finally, there is Aunt Sophie in Serbia, and married to a Partisan. So, it's just us for now."

"Yes uncle, I see all of that."

"Is there anyone that we can trust then?"

"Can I trust Zsofia Horthy, Uncle Stefan?"

"You need to be careful there, young man. Don't let your heart rule your head. If she and you ever get engaged to marry, then you should first talk to her about putting Germany first. But until she commits to that, please keep our secret from her."

"I will, Uncle Stefan. I will."

"You know that the Arrow Cross people rescued me from Czechoslovakia, and got me here. It was not easy for them to do. They are impressed with my medal and war stories. And I am impressed with their passion for Germany. They do their best to protect our heroes from the Soviets and others who want vengeance."

"That's important to do, Uncle Stefan."

"Would you like to come to the next meeting, Adam?"

Nikolaus was enjoying a late evening meal with his family, Magdolna, Miklos Jr., Countess Ilona, Zsofia, and Nicolette, when Paul Theer came to their quarters and knocked on its front door. He asked to be admitted even considering the hour.

"I don't wish for you to be alarmed, but we have become aware of a plot to attack you and your family. In particular, they want to kill or capture you, your son and the Countess. Everyone else is low priority, but they'll kill as many as they can. We have increased our security measures and called for additional personnel. You need to take extra precautions for now, so we needed to inform you all."

"Do you have any names? I could make a guess. Ferenc Szalasi comes to mind."

"Does it matter? Sorry, but we don't want to confirm or deny, and risk our sources."

"Okay. Just tell us what you want us to do."

"Just stay here at the villa, where we can protect you. No public events and no traveling around. Also, only one or two visitors at a time. No parties. No large groups. And don't assume that just because you were friends with someone, that they can't have been turned against you."

"It's nice here, isn't it? Cool by the stream and private for us behind these trees. May I kiss you, Zsofy? On the lips? Just tilt your head like this."

"Oh, Adam."

They hid, lying together in the tall grass. They both enjoyed the kissing and began to tentatively explore more of each other's bodies. For each of them, everything was new, forbidden and beautiful. They realized that they were in love. Their future seemed to stretch out before them. Love would overcome. Now for the hard part. They had to stop.

The day was not long coming when he asked if she would marry him and she accepted. He approached her father, with Zsofy giving him a little push from behind in the small of his back. His voice quivered, but he got out, "Mr. Horthy, I need to talk to you. I've fallen in love with Zsofy and would like your permission to marry her."

It was no great surprise for Miklos. The flirting had become bolder and more obvious. He had been close to his daughters as they grew and knew them well. And now he would be able to stop worrying that "something" would happen. "Yes Adam, you have my permission to ask my daughter for her hand in marriage." As though that hadn't already been done. But the ritual was played out.

Adan told his mother, and she was thrilled with the thought of Zsofia Horthy as her daughter-in-law. Magdalena and Anna told him that they couldn't be happier, for him and his new bride-to-be. Paul wasn't the romantic type. He only saw the security problems on the wedding day as an added complication.

Countess Ilona wasn't happy for more than one reason. First, she felt that Zsofia was marrying beneath her station. Next, with the grandmother's poor health, she would be expected to help Zsofia with the wedding details. And that would take up a lot of time. And then, sources in her social circle told her that Adam had attended a recent Arrow Cross meeting with Stefan. It was only one meeting, but she had a bad feeling, and didn't trust Stefan at all.

And neither was Nicolette happy. She thought, *"I'm so jealous that I could spit! And on top of that, I will have no choice but to accept her offer to be maid-of-honor."*

BEGINNINGS

The August day was showery in the morning, but cleared to bright and beautiful by early afternoon. Most of the groomsmen were, even then, still hungover. As were a couple of the bridesmaids, including Nicolette.

The service, on the lawn of the villa, was relatively small, but beautiful none-the-less. Archbishop Alexander officiated and brought the Pope's message and blessing. Countess Ilona had outdone herself.

Many of the guests lingered after Adam and Zsofy Diplich left on their honeymoon. They were escorted down the narrow dirt road by two jeeps full of MPs. Paul had seen to it that security was tight. He had not missed any detail. As the day ended and guests made their goodbyes, he finally began to relax.

Paul's charges, Miklos Sr., Magdolna, Miklos, Jr., Nicolette, the Countess and her five-year old Istvan, Jr. were all finally to bed by 10:00 in their secondfloor quarters. Nicolette had been half-carried to her room, and would, for the second morning in a row, be hungover.

Everything was also quiet on the first floor. Anna, and baby Elizabeth were already asleep. Magdalena was in her room with her toddler, Matty. Paul had seen Theresia, the groom's mother, finally give in to sleep and retire a few minutes ago. But he had lost track of Stefan, which was nothing new. Stefan could fend for himself, with that Walther that he always wore.

Paul took a walk around the villa checking that everything was in order and that the MP night shift was fully manned and in place. It was a beautiful starry night and he took a moment to look at the sky. Then he headed for bed.

Molly, his Miniature Schnauzer, was on the bed waiting for him to pet her for a few minutes. Then she would go into her unlocked crate for the night. She had her routine and even someone's wedding wouldn't change it.

Even though he was beat from the day, he couldn't sleep as deeply as he normally would and was awake at 2:30 AM. He heard a dog bark in the distance, but then go silent. Molly gave a low growl from her crate, got up and went to the door. Then another low growl.

Paul thought, *"Did I forget to let her out before going to bed? Might as well get up and take her out, since I can't sleep anyway. I'll walk around a bit, with her. That might help me sleep."*

He put on his pants and a light jacket over his pajamas. He slipped on his walking-shoes and placed his gun-belt around his waist, from force of habit. "Come on girl. But be quiet. Let's not wake up the whole house. Here, let me get your leash on. I'll turn on my flashlight and we'll go down the hall. Me and my 'good girl'. We'll see if the Moon is up."

Paul thought, *"Molly is a sweet dog. And smart as anything. But high-strung and quirky. She makes me laugh. The only thing is, she has a bark that would wake the dead. When anyone from outside the villa comes in, she gets excited and runs around barking so much that you can't hear yourself think. Paul thinks that's so funny, it makes me laugh. I love this dog!"*

"Molly, we've only gotten a few steps outside, and you've already found something to sniff. That's it, just freeze and don't budge. Come on girl."

A low growl. A glance back at me. *"She wants to know if I see it. But I don't. Something's not right out here. Turn off your flashlight. Draw your revolver. Don't move, just listen."*

A cough. Molly growls and starts to bark. Now really loud! Then 'zing'.

"Someone just shot at her! Son-of-a-bitch! Thank God, they missed. Little report. Silencer. Drop and lay flat. Let go of her leash. There she goes, into the dark. The unmistakable sound of an M-42 machine-gun right over my head. Crawl for the door. I have to get inside and get my people down into the bunker, to safety! Two shots from a pistol, I think."

Lights go on and MPs are shouting. A grenade explodes.

"Run for the door. Slam it behind me. Turn on my flashlight. Lock the door. Up the stairs and check doors. Most are open. As trained, my people have already run for the reinforced stairwell and down to the bunker in the basement. One door is still closed. It's locked. Nicolette's room. She's still inside.

"No response to my pounding. Probably passed-out drunk. Shoot the lock off the door. There she is. Even that didn't wake her up. Drag her off the bed and get her over my shoulder. Down the stairs. Through the short hallway. Good, the vault-like bunker door is still open. Pass her inside to her family. Close the bunker door. Close the bullet-proof outer door. Get the Thompson sub-machinegun out and put it by the gun-port. Turn on the intercom to inside the bunker."

"Sound-off!"

"One, two, three, five, six, seven."

"All of the Horthys except Zsofy, number four, and she's off site with Adam and the MPs. Very good!"

"Eight, nine, ten, eleven, twelve."

"All of my family except Adam, thirteen, and Stefan, fourteen. Excellent! But I just don't know about Stefan. Was that him with his Walther taking out the machine-gun? Don't know, but maybe."

"Fifteen, sixteen, seventeen, eighteen."

"Good, all the rest of the household staff."

Paul tells them, "No matter what happens out here, do not open your door! Do not open the door for anyone without the password. Do you remember it? 'Apatin' You're safe and can last indefinitely in there. Help will come soon enough. The MPs will have called for reinforcements."

Paul runs it through his head, *"Can the MPs handle the attack?*

Iffy. This is well planned. Probably had the positions of our men. Bastards. I have to be ready to defend this door for a while. And even if I don't make it through this, they're safe inside. That bunker can withstand just about anything. It was built by experts. And I have a few tricks, waiting for anyone who tries to reach it."

Time passes. *"Stay alert now."*

"The red-light blinked once. Someone just passed through the invisible beam at the bottom of the stairs. And again. And again. And a fourth time. Put on my gas-mask. Put on my ear protectors. Let's play a little music for them. Hit the control switch and the hallway is flooded with ear-piercing sound waves. Four blinks of the light as they retreat. Let them think about that for a while."

More time passes. *"Check my watch. 07:00 hours. Where is the cavalry? Can't hear what's going on up above. Got to fix that for the future."*

The red-light blinks once.

Someone calls out in German, "We've come to rescue you."

I respond, "Password".

The red-light blinks once.

"09:00. Something is wrong. Nobody had a chance to send a message that we were being attacked. Otherwise, help would be here by now. Not good. Take off the mask and ear-protectors. Have a snack and try to keep your energy high. Use the toilet, while you can. Make some coffee. Have a ration packet- good chocolate. Have a smoke and wait. Better put my equipment back on. They'll try again soon."

The light starts to blink multiple times.

"Sound waves on. Tear gas on. Oil mist on. That will fog their masks and make everything nice and slippery. Okay Mister Thompson, it's your turn. One clip. That's good. Now another for good luck. That should do it. Save your ammo."

No lights blink.

13:30. "Paul, it's Mr. Green. Come on out. Paul, don't you hear me. It's all over. I have your dog. Don't you want her?"

"What's the password?"

"Wedding."

"That's right. Come on down."

"He'll drop a grenade for sure and then come down to check the damage. Door is designed to take that. Just wait for the blast. There it is. Door held. Okay, now wait."

Light blinks once.

"Now use Mister Thompson again."

No lights blink.

"14:45. Nothing for a while. Let me check in with Anna and the rest. All of them, probably could use an update. They trained me to stay off the intercom and avoid any distractions but no one anticipated that it would be this long."

"How is everyone doing?"

"We are all good. No problems." Miklos Jr.'s voice.

"You probably wonder what's going on out here. We've had a few attempts to get in, but nothing's worked for them. The MPs are not here yet for some reason, but I'm confident that they will be soon. Just over twelve hours since the attack. Anna, how are you and Lizzy?"

"We were thinking about opening the door to find out what's going on. We are glad to hear from you. Here's Anna, she wants to say hello."

"Oh Paul, it's so good to hear that you're not hurt or anything. I was so worried. We're all just fine. A little crowded but very comfortable otherwise."

"Now, not too much talking. I need to keep it short. They might have listening devices and be able to hear us talk. I'll keep you updated more often. See you soon."

"15:30. Two pistol shots outside. What was that about?"

"Hello, Paul. It's Stefan. The password is 'Apatin'. Open up and come out. Is everyone okay? Does anyone need help?"

"Okay, we're coming out. It will take a few minutes. Have to rinse the hallway and get the doors open."

They came out of the bunker single-file, went around the five bodies and up the stairs to the ground level of the villa. Stefan was there waiting for them. He had Molly with him. She barked at everyone as they came out of the stairwell. When Stefan let go of her leash she ran to Paul and gave him a big greeting.

Paul thought *"I just love this dog! And Stefan's okay too."*

"Thanks for joining me for lunch Stefan. As I mentioned there are a few questions that we have about the attack, that we need to clear up."

"Sure Paul. No reason that you shouldn't have all the details as I understand them. I had hoped that the heads-up I gave you, would have resulted in a better outcome for the MPs who were on duty. My condolences. I know from personal experience; how tough it is to have men die under your command. And that now you need answers."

"Let's start at the beginning, with the attack. Was that you who took out the machine-gun and saved my ass?"

"Yes. That was me. It was fortunate that I was in the right position to do it. Took my best guess as to when they would come and the right spot to be at, and they both proved right."

"Where do you stand now with those Arrow Cross? On one hand, your actions when they attacked us have to mean that you're against them. Yet you attend their meetings, recruit new members to join and participate in many of their activities."

"It was the extremists in the organization that planned and carried out the attack, in secret from everyone else. I try and discourage such things from the inside. They do many good things for Germany and its veterans of war, widows and orphans. You know the organization is evolving now to be a political party. I am a German. This country welcomed us in when Hungary didn't want any more of us. Kicked us in the ass out the door. So, I want a strong Germany. The Allies want to keep us weak. But this war was proof in the long run what a mistake it was to try that."

"Okay. I don't agree, but it is a logical position."

"More logical perhaps than spending MPs' lives so that one criminal can testify against another criminal. You know that Veesenmayer will get off in the end anyway because he was a diplomat carrying out the instructions of his government. I would not have interfered except my family needed my help."

"We assume that all the MPs on duty were killed in the initial attack."

"Yes, that's right. They knew all of their positions and planned very well."

"It was about six hours between the first and second attacks on the bunker. Was that because of the sound waves?"

"Yes, that was very effective and slowed them down until they could go and find the right ear-protectors."

"Okay, but then another six hours plus, until the one man tossing a grenade. What was going on? Why so long and then only one?"

"They were arguing about whether to give it another try. Most thought that it was useless and wanted to leave. But one wanted to attack again. They decided that he should try on his own and come back up if he had any success with the grenade. When he didn't come back, all but two left. They set up a hidden position and were waiting for the Horthys to come out. I had to take them out myself."

"That all makes sense. Thank you."

"What's for lunch?"

Even after the war ended, the Hungarian POWs were not released immediately by the Russians. Then one morning in July, 1947, Ludwig and the rest of his Company of five-hundred men was loaded onto the same Studebaker trucks that had brought them to the camp. They were told for the first time, "The war is over. You are going home."

They reached Ukhta on the evening of the second day. After being fed, they slept in the open. The train came through the next morning. It was three days to Moskva, with a meal provided in soup kitchens at the end of each day. The trains stopped moving overnight and the men slept in the passenger-style cars.

In Moskva, they changed trains and headed for the eastern part of Hungary. This train traveled overnight and they arrived in the early evening of the second day. Overall it had taken six and one-half days.

They were processed in a camp outside of Debrecen, Hungary. It was for the soldiers, who had been captured by the Soviets at the Don River. They included 7,171 junior officers, 9,984 non-commissioned officers and 72,751 rank and file. On the first morning they were being issued identification documents.

"What is your name soldier?"

"Ludwig Genser."

"And do you remember your unit? Don't worry if you can't. We know it's been a while. We can still find you in the records if you can't remember. It will just take a little longer."

"I remember. It was 2nd Army, III Corp, Light Division 6. I forget my század number though."

"No problem, I'll find you in the Division rolls. Just wait here a few minutes and I'll be right back."

Only five-minutes passed. "I found you. No problem. Is your brother with you?"

"No, he was killed in action. Then we ran out of ammunition and the few of us remaining were captured."

"I see. We, and I personally, are sorry for your loss. My uncle went missing in that battle. I saw that you are listed as being from Apatin. I'm afraid that I have bad news for you."

"What!?" Ludwig said with sudden fear in his heart.

"Apatin is now in the new country of Yugoslavia, with Serbia, Croatia and others. They have forcibly emptied the Swabian villages, in the whole of Batschka, and either put the people into work camps or deported them to West Germany. Many have lost everything in the forced exodus.

Hungary has suffered so much, the Soviet occupation, towns and countryside devastated from the fighting, and the worst hyperinflation in history, the money is worthless. And there are still some three-hundred-thousand of its troops languishing in Soviet POW camps.

I'm afraid that Hungary will blame all Germans, even those that fought for Hungary, and also deport them to West Germany. It would be best if you just went there now. And you might be able to locate your family there. In any event, you can never go home."

"But, . . . but. . . ." Ludwig didn't know what to say.

The only member of his family that they could locate was his cousin, Stefan Butscher living near Weilheim, West Germany. He was taken by truck to Budapest. There the Red Cross gave him train tickets from Budapest to Vienna and from Vienna to Munich.

So, he was walking the fifty kilometers from Munich to Weilheim. He looked like a skeleton in ragged clothes as he walked down the hot and dusty road. It was around Noon, and the sun was already blasting down.

The MP on duty said, "Get out of here! We have nothing for you. Keep moving on you bum. You stink to high heaven."

"Do you know where Stefan Butscher lives? I know that he's around here somewhere."

"What would you want with him? How do you even know his name? Who gave it to you."

"I'm his cousin and the Red Cross gave it to me."

"I never heard of any long-lost cousin. Get out of here before you get shot."

"Tell whoever is in charge that I'm Ludwig Genser from Apatin. I need someone to help me find my cousin Stefan."

"Yeah, you better not be lying. We had trouble around here not too long ago and don't cotton to anyone that we don't know getting any closer to this house. So just stand still and I'll check. But I'll shoot you if you try to come up this driveway. Understand?"

It wasn't long before Theresia came running out of the villa and down the driveway. "Ludwig! Ludwig! Get out of my way. Let him in. Let him in. He's family."

Ludwig cried for the first time in three-and-a-half years. "Cousin Theresia, I was searching for Stefan and I've found you. What a happy surprise! Is Stefan here? Are the others here? Do you know where my mother is?"

"Stefan is here, but drove off this morning to town. He'll be so happy to see you this afternoon, when he gets back. My son Adam and his new wife *Zsofy, one of the* Horthys, are here; as are your cousin Konrad's wife, Magdalena and her son Mathias; Konrad lives in East Berlin now; and Magdalena's sister, Anna, and her husband Paul Theer, an American diplomat, and their little girl, Elizabeth are all here. So, we are one big happy family, working for the Hortys."

"And my mother? You didn't say anything about my mother! Please, you can't tell me anything bad."

"No, no, as far as we know, she's fine. She still lives in Apatin, with her Husband, Josip Stambolic. You didn't know that she was married now? He's a big-shot with the Communist government there in Yugoslavia. We wrote her a few times after we heard that you were alive. But we never received an answer, so we just think that the letters didn't get through to her. But, we are sure that Josip would have written to us if there was any bad news. He was the one who got Konrad and Stefan out of there just in time."

"Come in now, come in. We have to get you cleaned up and some new clothes."

"First, I'd like some water please. I'm so thirsty."

He had to start eating slowly. His stomach couldn't handle much food. But soon that improved and he started to gain a little weight. But his mind was troubled by flashbacks to the terrible winter fighting, his brother's death and then his captivity. It would be a long time, if ever, until he found peace.

Stefan made it his goal to help Ludwig. One thing that he did was to invite Ludwig to attend the Arrow Cross meetings. They had established a veterans' recovery group that held monthly round-table sharing sessions.

It was March, 1948 before the International Military Tribunal at Nuremberg was ready to hear testimony against Edmund Veesenmayer, ex-Ambassador of Nazi Germany to Hungary. Paul led a heavy security convoy transferring Ex-Regent Horthy to the prison there. Horthy was one of the principal witnesses concerning the deportations to Auschwitz four years earlier in the Spring of 1944. Veesenmayer was found guilty and sentenced to 20 years in prison. After serving less than three years, he was released.

Horthy returned to the villa near Weilheim. A full security detail of MPs was deemed no longer necessary. Paul and three contractors hired by the State

Department filled that function until the Horthys moved to Portugal in 1950. None of the Butschers, Theers, Diplichs or Gensers went with them.

BERLIN

"Cold, windy and rainy again. But in the city's lights, the recently repaired Leipziger Strasse shines like glass. Pretty. But I'm lonely here in Berlin, staring out my office window. All that I ever wanted was my family and my farm in Hungary. But there is no going home to that now. I, Konrad Butscher, am a top technocrat of the Deutsche Wirtschaftskomission (DWK)—the German Economic Commission. What a good joke on me."

The DKW had just assumed administrative authority in the Soviet zone.

"Around the corner and three blocks south is the American's Checkpoint Charlie. Put that thought out of your head Konrad. The only question is, how many blocks you'd get before the Stasi caught up with you. It's only been a month, and I miss Maggie so much already. And my five-year old son, Mathias, it's just as bad. He misses his father and I miss him to death. I'll never get back this time that I should have been with him."

Rain beats against the window. It's time to do something.

"Could Maggie and Mathias get through the travel restrictions, just imposed by the Soviets? Would they try? Telephone-service is cut off. Mail is being censored. You have to be careful what you say or write. How could I know if they were already on the way? I could strand them here, if I made it across the border at the same time that they came the other way."

There was no chance to answer the perfunctory knock on the office door before the DWK Chairman, Heinrich Rau, and his aide walked in. "I'm glad that you're still here *Comrade Butscher*. We need to go over your plans for the Reichsmark. Feel free to speak your mind in front of Comrade Heidi. She is good at keeping my confidences. Let's sit down and I'll update you on what's happened."

"Sit here at the table. We will be more comfortable. Can I get you a drink?"

"English whiskey, if you have it, with just a splash of water. Just enough to prevent fire, ha, ha."

"Yes, I've been saving a bottle. And yours, Comrade Heidi?"

"She doesn't drink while she's working."

And I thought to myself, *"Just probing. I'd heard the rumors that she was a well-trained killer, assigned to Rau as his protection; or perhaps his mistress; or perhaps his keeper."*

"Have one yourself. You can relax. Let's get started."

"What's going on?"

Chairman Rau started by saying, "Your little games are over. Now everyone knows about them. Gold in Swiss banks, diamonds in Soviet Embassies in Johannesburg and Washington, deeds to Texas oil wells at our United Nations office in New York, drilling equipment at work in Saudi Arabia, art-works in the Soviet Embassy in Paris. Have I missed anything? It's quite a list."

He continued, "We are very happy with your work. You should be complimented on how you've played with the value of the Reichsmark. Printing all that paper-money, and then using each devaluation to screw with the commodities markets around the world. But they are on to you now. They've figured it out. You can't get away with anything else."

And I'm thinking, *"Good, no mention of the deed to the Inn at the ski-resort in Lake Placid."*

"Some of our Comrades think that you are too much of a Cap-italist. Are you?"

"Everything that I've done was for the Proletariat." I replied.

"That's what I told them."

"Who is 'them'?"

"Don't ask such questions. Let's not talk any longer about the past. Our concern this evening is about the present and future."

"Okay. What's going on."

The Chairman went on, "We've heard that the Americans and the British are trying to bring in a new German currency. It's a ploy to re-align Europe in their vision. Obviously, Stalin is against that. We met with Soviet Foreign Minister Molotov today and were told that we're not going to let their unilateral decision stand. They want an economically stable and strong Germany and we want to keep her weak and in recession. They and the French are playing games; consolidating their occupation zones, and then extending the American 'Marshall Plan' to its new government. At our meeting Molotov said, 'What happens to Berlin, happens to Germany; what happens to Germany, happens to Europe.' I'm sure that those are Stalin's thoughts exactly and you know what happens to those who don't fully implement his wishes."

I leaned forward and looked him in the eye, "Since coming here to Berlin, I've made his wishes my only concern. And the answer to this development is relatively straight-forward. We just keep printing and circulating our own Reichsmark and not recognize theirs at all."

"The Soviets have another answer. As you've probably heard, their military is 'regulating' access to and from Berlin in order to starve them out. Don't worry, we'll get passes to your wife, so that she and your son can visit you. But you two must realize that real trouble could start at any time from this military standoff. If there is a confrontation, we don't know what the Americans will do. There is even talk about the atomic bomb being used by them, since their garrison is so weak."

"Well, I'll certainly do my part, and keep the spigots open on our currency. And remember, we just don't honor any new currency from them. And, I'll warn my wife, and she can decide about coming here, during these troubles. But in any event, the military situation won't be allowed to affect my work."

"Very good, Comrade Butscher." With that, Chairman Rau stood, said his goodbyes and headed out the door with Comrade Heidi following close behind. Leaning back to close the door behind her, she smiled and winked at me.

The Allies began to supply their forces in Berlin by air. Soviet military aircraft began to violate West Berlin airspace and buzz flights in and out. On April 5th, a fighter collided with a British passenger jet and all aboard both crafts were killed. Tensions rose.

In May, the Soviet Union directed its military to put in circulation its own new currency. It was introduced on June 22nd as the exclusive one permitted in Berlin subject to economic penalties. Konrad had no involvement and stopped printing the now outdated Reichsmark.

But the Allies had already introduced a new Deutsche Mark (DM) on June 21st, in the three sectors that they controlled. They had flown two-hundred fifty million DMs into Berlin secretly. With its stable value, it quickly became the standard currency throughout all four zones, including the Soviet's.

After three months of waiting, the promised travel passes hadn't reached Maggie. Now the only way into Berlin was by air, but that was dangerous and the airfare was expensive. Still, she had to see Konrad and tell him that in November, he would be a father again.

Then the Soviets launched well-advertised military maneuvers right outside of the city and rumors spread of an occupation of the Allies' sectors. In response, the Allies stopped all rail traffic into East Germany.

That was a serious blow to its economy. Then the Soviets

blockaded all Western surface traffic into Berlin. The Allies began the "Berlin Airlift" on June 24th, which would last for just under eleven months.

✯ ✯ ✯

"Do you like me in this little summer-dress that I just bought to please you? I wanted to; please you that is. See anything that you'd like to have? I've seen you looking. We could find a quiet place to have dinner and then you could come over to my apartment. It's not far." Comrade Heidi purred.

"No thank you. I love my wife."

"So what? I don't care. You can keep her. But in the meanwhile, since you're alone here, you should relax and have some fun with me."

"No, no, you're very pretty and all, but I'll pass."

"Well Konnie, if you change your mind, just tell me. I'll be around and available for you."

After Comrade Heidi left his office, Konrad thought, *"I'm in trouble. Without control of the currency, my usefulness to them is almost gone. That was just an attempt to compromise me. I can't wait any longer. I have to take the chance and run."*

But a good chance was not easy to come by. And not only Comrade Heidi, and the rest of her Stasi, but the Russian NKVD was keeping an eye on him.

They, the Russians, had assigned two fairly good accountants to go over his books. They hadn't found anything. Not yet, but Lake Placid was hidden in there. It was only a matter of time, until someone found the discrepancy.

"To start, I'll make it my practice to walk around the block every afternoon. And at home I'll practice running at night in my dress shoes. If anyone asks I'll tell them that it helps me get back to sleep."

Shortly after, Chairman Rau and Comrade Heidi came to his office again. A perfunctory knock and in they walked.

"Good morning Comrade Butscher. Hope that we are not disturbing you. May we sit here at your desk? One day I'll have to find out what you do, all morning by yourself, in here. Anyway, that's not what we came for. How is everything going with the introduction of the new money that we got from the Russians?"

"Not bad really. Slower than we might have hoped due to the new DM that the West introduced just the day before ours. I'm pushing very hard to have our banks, larger stores, service providers and city government offices only do business with our money. But all that I ever hear from them is that everyone deals in the DM, so they too have to accept it."

"Not acceptable!!" Rau pounded my desk. "You are required to make this go our way and not theirs. This is critical. Spend all your time and efforts on it. There will be hell to pay for both of us if it doesn't.

Maybe you are too soft and not the right man for this kind of thing? Not a real man, if you know what I mean." And Comrade Heidi gave me a wink, but no smile.

It was mid-afternoon on a warm summer day. Leaving my suit jacket behind, I walked down the stairs and went out onto the *Leipziger Strasse.* Automobile traffic light. Some pedestrians, but not crowded. There was a shaved-ice vender and I stopped and ordered one, as was my routine.

In my left-rear pocket, was my identification documents. In my right-rear, the deed to the Lake Placid inn. My rosary, comb and handkerchief were all that I had in the other pants pockets. I was wearing the dress-shoes that I had practiced running in.

"I'll just walk to the corner and take a look. It looks clear. I'll walk the first block eating my ice, and then make a run if there are still no Stasi in sight. How can I tell them from just anyone? Fool! Anybody you see has to be Stasi. Who else would be out on the last two blocks? I'm at the corner. Should I try it?—Should I try it?—"

Air-raid sirens begin to wail.

"Is it the Americans and their atomic bomb? Everyone is on edge. People, even the border-guards, run for their shelters. Now is the time! Run for the checkpoint. Run hard!"

After 30 seconds, the sirens stop. It was just a test. There's a yell from behind.

"Stop, Butscher, stop!"

"One block down, one to go. Even at this distance, I know her voice. What had Stefan taught me? Zig-zag. It will throw off the shooter's aim. I can hear the first bullet going past. Lucky, she just has a pistol. Another shot. That was close. 100 meters to go. I can hear the American soldiers urging me on."

A bullet smashes the glass of an American soldier's sentry-hut. He comes out and raises his rifle to firing position. But he doesn't shoot.

"I'm down! Did I trip? Am I hit? Now there's pain in my right leg. It hurts like hell. I can't get up. Crawl. Crawl. Soldiers run out and start pulling me the last twenty-five meters. I'm across the line. I'm safe now. Thank God. What's happening to me? I feel myself passing out."

The American military hospital is clean and well run.

The nurses are very professional. But, not all speak German very well. That's alright, some do. I'm being well cared for, this past day, since I woke up. The right leg is there, but in a cast, and raised so that it's above the level of my heart.

I say a little prayer of thanks to God, and wait for the interrogations to start. They will have to establish who I am and why I took such a chance. I'm floating, . . . from time to time. It must be morphine. Sleep comes again, so easily. This is nice.

"Good morning Konrad. Wake up. Wake up." And so, another day starts. The leg hurts but not too bad. The morphine is being cut back, I'm sure. It was nice while it lasted. The nurses start their daily morning routine. My papers must have been checked since they know my name.

Later that morning a man comes in. "Good morning, Konrad Butscher. You gave everyone quite a scare. That bullet hit an artery and you almost bleed out, before we got you here. Doctors say that your fine now and that it's just a matter of healing. I'm Paul Brown. And I need to ask you some questions."

"Alright, I think, I'm up for talking to you."

"Is Konrad Butscher your real name?"

"Yes."

"Do you know that someone tried to get in, and we think, kill you, right here in this hospital? She might have done it too, if our metal detector didn't go off, when she came up to this security floor."

"Really! Did you catch her?"

"No, she was too fast. Ran out down the stairs. A car was waiting for her and she got away. But we have her picture. Here. Do you recognize her?"

"Yes, by the name, Comrade Heidi. I don't have a last name, but the rumor was that she's a well-trained assassin. I think that she's with the Stasi or maybe even the NKVD. No one was sure."

"We've decided to get you out of here today and fly you to our airbase at Baden-Baden, West Germany. It's a little sooner than we had planned to move you, but you'll be safer there."

"Where are my clothes and the things that were in my pockets?"

"Don't worry. Your clothes are ruined, but we'll get new stuff for you. We have all of the things from your pockets. The deed on the Lake Placid Inn is very interesting. That's where the Winter Olympics were held in 1932. I took the train up from New York City when I was young. You'll have to tell me how you came away with a deed on that, from here in Berlin."

"It's a long story, but it's something that fell through the cracks on a deal that came along for antiquities out of Egypt. The art dealer lost a bet." "A deal on antiquities out of Egypt? What exactly were you doing for Communist Germany and is that why they're trying to kill you now? A well-trained assassin is not easy to come by, so you must be fairly important. Right?"

"I have a talent for mathematics and for a while I was in charge of the money supply. The Russians wanted to keep Germany weak and have me keep printing and putting into circulation more and more Reichsmarks. So, it was easy for me to manipulate the commodities market and acquire hard assets for them. But the markets caught on to that and at almost the same time the new DMs came into circulation. My usefulness was ending and it was time to get out."

"Now they want you dead, in order to keep you from spilling the beans."

"Yes, spilling the beans. I have to learn these little American phrases."

"And what do you know about running an Inn?"

"Oh, my family owned one in Apatin, in Hungary. That was until the war came along and changed everything. My wife told me during a visit that the communists took that inn away from my parents and sent them to a workcamp. I felt that it was only fair that we get another inn as compensation."

"That information confirms for me, that you are truly Konrad Butscher. You'll be surprised to learn that I'm your brother-in-law, the Paul who's married to Anna, your wife's sister."

"Oh, really? Now that is a pleasant surprise. It's keeping everything in the family. Isn't it? Well welcome to the family, Paul. Sorry that I couldn't be there for the wedding."

✳ ✳ ✳

On June 18, 1948, the National Security Council had issued Directive 10/2 calling for covert action against the USSR, and granting the authority to carry out those operations to the newly formed Central Intelligence Agency.

Konrad was flown to Baden-Baden in an Air Force general's well-appointed C-47. He was fully de-briefed by Paul and other agents of the CIA over the coming weeks.

Maggie and Mathias visited him there, before the debriefings were completed. Maggie was clearly showing.

"I have good news for you Konrad. You are going to be a father again. I'm expecting in November. Remember when I visited you last February?"

"That is great news! Matty can use a little brother or sister, so that he will not be so spoiled. And I will be there for those early years with the new baby. Those that I missed so much with Matty, while we were separated."

When Konrad was well enough, in late July, to be released from the hospital, he was driven under guard to the villa in Weilheim. He was allowed to keep the deed to the inn. The CIA felt that it made things safer and much easier for him to have a business in the States. Stefan and Paul agreed that round-the-clock security was again necessary. Two contractors were stationed there until Konrad, Maggie and Matty could emigrate to the United States.

SOPHIE'S WALK

The August sun beats down on the heavily dressed woman walking down the dirt road. It's obvious to anyone who cares to look, that she is dirty, bedraggled, her hair is cropped short and she's missing her front teeth. She swings a long stick from side-toside as she walks. It does not allow anyone to get near. She mumbles to herself in a loud voice.

Then she stops and yells, "Where are my boys? Do you know my boys? Ludwig and Filipp are their names. Do you know me? That's right, just ignore me. Like I'm not here. I see you. You hear me! Another one with no words. How rude all of you are." Some distance on, she repeats herself.

Her journey had started with her husband's assassination and then her beating and humiliation. She and Mathias, her brother-in-law, fled across the Danube at Erdut; went west through Osijek; and then south to the Sava River Valley. Following that valley, they went through Zagreb, Ljubljana and Hrusica.

North of Hrusica, as they approached the Drava River, two men tried to rape her. Mathias fought and hit one over the head with a rock. Then the other man stabbed him and that cost him his life. He just fell by the side of the road and couldn't get up. He died two hours later, just bled out. His last act, was to give her the letter to his children.

At the little town of Villach, Austria she got help to carry him to the nearest church. The village priest agreed to put him in an unmarked grave in the church's cemetery. That was mostly just to get rid of the "crazy woman", who wouldn't leave until he agreed to bury the stranger. As he gave his blessing, she was the only one at the graveside. The two pines, at the front of the church, moaned in the wind.

After his burial, she followed the Drava up to its tributary the Isel River, then its tributary the Tavernb River and from there across the Alps.

Fortunate for her, that her crossing was during late July.

At the castle in Hirschberg, from where Theresia's last letter had been posted, Sophia was told, "Move on you dirty scarecrow! No one wants you around here. Look for your family in Weilheim in Oberbayern. That's where the whole bunch of those Hungarian Swabians have gone. You and your family are not welcome here. Now move along!"

The letter had finally come through, just before Josip was shot and killed. It contained the news that at least her son Ludwig was alive. She would not rest now, until she was with him again. That was all that gave her the will to continue walking. She had covered over nine-hundred kilometers.

She continued on. One foot after the other and finally reached the locked gate of the villa. The MPs were gone now that Horty's testimony at Nuremberg was complete. The contractors had taken over.

She yelled at the villa, and kept yelling, "Where are my boys? Do you know my boys, Ludwig and Filipp? Do you know me? Will anyone answer me?"

Stefan came to the gate. "You can't just keep standing there yelling." He looked a second time and realized who it was. "Aunt Sophie! It's you. What have they done to you? Come and let me help you."

"Do you know me? Are my boys here? Please tell me."

"Yes, I know you Aunt Sophie. I'm Stefan. Look closely at me. Take your time. Do you recognize me now? We will take care of you. You're home now. You're with your family." He took her into his arms and held her close.

"Stefan, I must tell you. Your mother and father have passed away. Your mother, years ago at the workcamp. And your father, just now during our walk as we tried to find you. He has written a letter to you, and Konrad and Theresia. I have it in my bag. He thought of you three right up until the end. He was stabbed and I had him buried at the church in Villach, Austria."

"That's terrible!"

"But tell me, tell me, who is here? Is my Ludwig here? Or do the Russians still have him? Is there any news about Filipp? What about the others in our family? I'm so full of fear for them all."

"Come in. Come in. Theresia is right inside. Ludwig is in the work-shed in back and I'll get him right away. Adam is married if you can imagine that. There is so much to tell you."

"Theresia look who's here. It's Aunt Sophie."

"I can't believe my eyes!" Hugging Sophie, Theresia said, "Praise to God! Praise to God! You're home. You're alive. You are safe. Look what they did to you! We will take care of you now. It's all over."

"Stefan, Theresia, you haven't mentioned Filipp. Is he here?"

"I'm afraid that Filipp is not here. I'll let Ludwig tell you about him. They were together at the end. But sit here at the table. You look so tired."

Just then Ludwig ran in and grabbed his mother. "It's you! I've missed you so much! Sobs. I thought that I'd never see you again. My prayers are answered. When it was so bad in Russia, so cold, you were the thought that kept me going."

"Ludwig, what's happened to your brother? Where is Filipp?"

"We were freezing to death. Just the eight of us had to attack the Russians' camp. We had to get out of the cold and get food. I thought that we would all die. Filipp was so brave, but he was killed. Then I was knocked unconscious and never saw him again."

Konrad, Maggie and Matty returned from Konrad's doctor visit. Paul and Anna and Liz soon joined them. Over the rest of the day they shared their stories, grieved those that had been lost and gave thanks to God for those that had survived.

"Your father was so brave. He protected me on the road in Austria. Here he wrote this letter before all that. It's to you Stefan and you Theresia and you Konrad. Anyway, I now give this letter to you, as was your father's dying wish."

Theresia read her father's letter first. "Sophie, you've been through so much. My heart aches for you. It was terrible the way Josip was murdered, and then being beaten and driven out like that. And forced to walk here with just the clothes on your back. Then my father killed defending you. It's all so sad." And Theresia began to weep.

Then Stefan read it. "My father was right about so many things. I'm very glad that he wrote this for us. But sad for you, for all the things you went through on your walk. You are a tough woman."

Konrad read it last. He read it closely. But he made no comment.

"Anna, good news. I've been called back to the States to work in our headquarters. You can become a Permanent Resident and take your papers out, to become a citizen. Elizabeth was born there, so she already is one. What do you think?"

"That would be great, but what about my family?"

"Magdalena and Konrad and Matty are a given. Headquarters wants him back there for his own safety and he already has a business in the States. I can get the paperwork on them, as Permanent Residents, without any problem. Stefan, Theresia, Sophie, Adam, Zsofy and Ludwig all have different issues and I'm not even sure which of them would want to go."

The next night at dinner, Adam was the first to voice a decision, "We have talked about it, and Zsofy and I have decided not to come. She does not want to leave her family at this time. We are now trying to have a baby and I agree with her that it is best to stay here."

Theresia then declared, "If that is their decision, I also want to stay here, so that I can be part of my grandchildren's lives."

Sophie said, "Well yes, I for one would definitely like to go! It would be such a wonderful thing to start over in a new place. A fresh start away from this destroyed place is just what I need."

When it was Ludwig's turn, he simply said, "I want to go with Stefan. Wherever he goes is fine with me, as long as I can also come."

And Stefan said, "It would be great to go, if you can get us Permanent Resident status, Paul. Is that a problem?"

"I'll have to see what I can do for you three."

No one guessed that Mathias Diplich had survived the siege of Castle Hill and was alive in Estonia. But Theresia's mother's intuition would not let her give up hope for him.

Sophia began to heal physically over the next weeks. A highly professional dentist in Munich was found to do bridgework and save those teeth that could be saved. He had a great deal of experience in dealing with injuries from the war.

Sophie's hair was growing in, although it was still too short to style. But at least it was cut evenly. She began to feel much better about her life. She was proud of her two sons, her two husbands and herself for the way that they had dealt with life's challenges. She was not one to waste her life in regrets.

It was a beautiful early fall morning in 1948, in Oberbayern. The weather was perfect for a walk. The trees were beginning to change color. Sophie decided to stroll along the Schlittbach, a stream flowing to the Zellsee. The stream flowed below the hill where the villa was located.

She took Paul's dog, Molly, with her. As dogs do, it kept pace with Sophie, running in circles around her at about 25 meters distance. Back and forth down through the fields, Molly loved walks like this and could go endlessly.

After about thirty minutes, Sophie noticed another woman coming fast along the path behind her. Since Sophie was just taking her time and the woman was walking at a crisp pace, the distance between them was closing.

Molly came to her, placed herself between them facing the stranger, and gave an uncharacteristic deep growl. Her ears went down, back arched and hair along her spine raised. Sophie had never seen her do something like that.

"You don't like that lady, do you? That's strange.

You always love the women. And Paul and Stefan told me to pay attention to you. Let's just cut across the field and back up to the villa. We'll see what she does."

As Sophie left the trail, and began the climb, on a straight line toward the villa, the stranger started to cut across on an angle that would intercept them. And the woman began to run. Sophie's legs were in good shape from all her walking. She knew that she was in trouble and began to sprint up the hill.

"Let's go Molly, we can't let her catch us. Go! Go!"

But Molly had a different idea. She turned off and headed straight at the woman. Molly was not a big dog, at ten kilos, but her attack was relentless. It forced the woman to come to a halt, draw her pistol and fire. The second shot hit Molly and third killed her. But a fragment from that third bullet ricocheted off a rock, and hit the shooter in her foot.

Meanwhile Sophie was putting enough distance between them that even an expert couldn't hope to hit her with a pistol shot. As she continued running, Sophie saw a car pull up at the villa's front gate and two men simultaneously get out of the rear doors. She stopped, unsure what to do next.

It was then, that Sophie saw Stefan step out from behind the wall at the front gate. She saw that he was holding a double-barrel shotgun. The men were at the rear of the car looking at her. Stefan said something to them that Sophie couldn't make out. They turned toward Stefan and started to draw their guns. It was the last thing they ever did. The car roared away.

The woman began to limp away across the field toward the trail. Stefan unhurriedly went inside and returned with a scoped T20E2, an experimental rifle supplied by the CIA. He chambered a bullet, took careful aim down the slope, and dropped the woman at two hundred and fifty meters, with the first shot.

Due to the cessation of the war only one hundred of these rifles had been produced by the Americans. They were intended for the invasion of Japan, which was never necessary. The CIA wanted to evaluate them in the field, in addition to the proving grounds, and were supplying them to a few experts around the world.

Sophie ran past the two bodies and into the villa. She called, "Konrad, Konrad, come! Stefan needs your help!" He was in the shower when the two shotgun blasts went off and was just dressed and coming down the stairs. He and Stefan dragged the two bodies out of sight.

They were both carrying Soviet TT-33 pistols. They are powerful weapons capable of penetrating soft body armor and able to withstand tremendous abuse. The Russian and their allied armies and police forces used them, so extensively, that they revealed nothing about the affiliation of these two men.

When they went down to the woman, Konrad recognized her immediately. Comrade Heidi lay dead twenty-five meters away from Molly. "This is the Comrade Heidi, that I've been telling you about. She tried again, but this time perhaps to kill or kidnap Sophie as a way to get at me. We'll never know exactly what she had planned."

Stefan checked her gun and found that it was a "suppressed" Nagant M1895 revolver. "Suppressed", meaning that it had what is commonly called a "silencer". Its barrel was cut down to aid in concealment. Stefan said, "This is an assassin's weapon. It's commonly used by the NKVD." He kept it for his own collection.

They carried the woman and Molly back up the hill. Stefan called Sophie and had her look at the dead woman's face. "Do you know her? There has to be some reason why she would take this kind of risk in order to kill you. Look closely at her face and see if you have any recollection."

Sophie looked and thought for a few minutes. "You know she does look familiar. I've seen her somewhere before. I'm good at this. I'll get it."

"Just don't force it. You'll remember better if you just let it come naturally."

Then Sophie remembered. "It was at the Inn at Apatin. She was with the Partisans when they captured the town in 1944. They all stayed at the Inn and then she paid us in Serbian Dinars. Made us take them even though they were worthless."

Stefan said to Konrad, "You know, she probably wasn't after you this time. She was after Sophie, I'm sure. Sophie probably wasn't meant to get away when they killed Josip. They have only now been able to find her. Maybe someone working for her dentist. The Serbs want her dead because she knows something. She might not even know, that she knows it. Or they just think that she knows it. Comrade Heidi may have been a double agent for the Serbs."

Konrad shook his head. "It's all too deep for me Stefan. I'm just glad that she's dead."

"I'll talk to Paul about the whole thing when he returns. Tomorrow, yes? In the meanwhile, you two still be careful. Whether it's you or Sophie, they could still send someone else. Stay inside the walls for now, until we figure it out."

The three bodies were put into a horse cart and covered with tarps. When it got dark they took them down to the main road and dumped them along its side. They were gone the next morning. The local police were never aware.

Molly was buried inside the little grove of trees, behind the main building.

Paul returned from a meeting in Frankfurt the next afternoon. "My Molly is dead? What happened? Shot by an assassin who was after Sophie? I need to hear everything that went on here yesterday."

After a full briefing by Sophie, Konrad and Stefan, Paul took a full minute to absorb it all. "One thing that it does, is to make it even more critical that we get you three back to the States. We need to fully debrief you before another attempt is made to kill one of you."

"What about my family?" Konrad asked.

"Everyone else who said they wanted to go will be brought over by ocean-liner. The doctors will have the final say for Maggie, but I see no reason that she can't follow immediately. We can book passage for all of them on a nice ship."

"Stefan asked, "And Ludwig?"

"He may be detained in a camp briefly, but yes, Ludwig will come with the rest of the family by ship. They just need to confirm his identity and story. They are working on that for me right now."

"What kind of camp, Paul?"

"German POW. Don't worry it's not like the Russians'."

"That is not going to be satisfactory. He is already having great problems adjusting after his experiences at that lumber-cutting work-camp, that he was in for over four years. Now you want to put him into another camp? That will not happen. You will get no more cooperation from me if it's even mentioned to him. Do you understand?" Stefan's determination was obvious.

"Oh, that's clear enough. I'll discuss what you said in detail with my superiors."

"You do that."

The C-69C Constellation sat on the runway at the Frankfurt Airbase. It was a 43-seat VIP transport, built in 1945 at the Lockheed-Burbank plant. After Paul escorted Konrad, Sophie, Stefan and Ludwig aboard and got them seated, the propellers of the four engines began turning one at a time. It would be a long flight to Langley Airbase outside of Washington, D.C.

The first game of 1948's World Series was starting in Boston with the announced pitchers being Johnny Sain for the National League Braves and Bob Feller for the Cleveland Indians. Paul, an avid baseball fan, was looking forward to seeing a game on the new television coverage from a station in Washington.

Anna, Elizabeth, Maggie and Matty were traveling by car to Amsterdam, Netherlands for a crossing on the luxurious liner Nieuw Amsterdam. It had taken fourteen months to restore her to her pre-war condition, and in October 1947 she had resumed her transatlantic schedule. Maggie had an appointment scheduled for two days after her arrival with an obstetric doctor in Manhattan.

Konrad couldn't wait to see his inn at Lake Placid, in the Adirondack Mountains of New York. He just had to get these Central Intelligence Agency debriefings over and start a normal life.

DEBRIEFINGS

The twenty-four-hour flight, included a stop in Iceland for refueling and then at "Ernest Harmon Air Force Base" in Stephenville, Newfoundland. That base was one of the largest U.S. military airfields located outside of the United States. It was a frequent stopping and refueling point for US military aircraft crossing the Atlantic.

From its establishment in 1941, this base existed as a de facto enclave of United States territory within the Dominion of Newfoundland. United States military personnel stationed here were therefore subject to the Uniform Code of Military Justice.

Escorted by Paul Theer of the CIA, Konrad Butscher, Stefan Butscher, Sophia Stambolic and Ludwig Genser met with an agent of the Immigration and Naturalization Service (INS) and received their Alien Registration Receipt Cards (INS Form I-151). These identification cards attest to a person's permanent resident status in the United States. Owing to its green design it is known informally as a "green card". The application process for a green card usually takes several years.

The plane was refueled and a crew change was made.

The CIA contractors who had flown the first leg were replaced by US Air Force personnel. Then the C-69C Constellation took-off for Langley Air Force Base in Virginia. It landed uneventfully and taxied to the terminal of the Military Air Transport Service. The party of five de-planed first.

They were met on the tarmac by four Air Force MPs.

After collecting their baggage, they walked through the terminal to its exit. There an additional CIA agent was waiting for them. At the curb were two Air Force staff-cars; blue four-door Pontiacs, chauffeured by additional MPs.

They were driven to 2430 E St. NW in the center of Washington, DC. The newly formed CIA had taken over this site from its wartime predecessor, the Office of Strategic Services. There was no sign on the building.

Once inside the front entrance the Air Force personnel left.

"These are nice rooms that they gave us." Sophie was standing at the open door of Ludwig's room.

"Nicest prison I've ever been in. The bed and furniture are first class. And look at the view over the garden wall of the Lincoln Memorial, the other buildings and the Potomac River. It's spectacular! I've never had better food from a mess-kitchen. And all the agents and other people couldn't be more gracious. But we're still in a prison. Haven't you noticed that we're confined to only one section of this building?"

"Well, we'll be out soon enough. They just want all the information that we can possibly supply them. Some of the stuff that they had me remembering! Well, I didn't even realize that those things were still in my head.

"What did they ask you about?"

"The first thing was about when Josip was killed. They wanted to know who did that to him. They showed me pictures of Serbian agents. There were four that came and killed him that day, but I was only able to identify one of them, from the pictures. That was it."

"Why are they interested in that?"

"I don't have any idea."

"What else?"

"Then it was about the woman that Konrad called Comrade

Heidi. That wasn't her real name, but they didn't say what it was. Did you know that one night at the Inn, she was pointed out to everyone, as the one in charge of the executions of the Swabian officers and soldiers from the Bor copper mine? You know, the POWs, that the Serbs captured, who were bringing the Jewish laborers to Hungary. The Partisans were bragging how she had those Swabians lined up on the side of the road, and then the whole bunch of them shot. They said that she did a lot of the shooting herself."

"Well she's dead. So why would they be interested?"

"I think that they're looking for other people in Yugoslavia who can be threatened with war crimes. You know that there were over two thousand Swabian POWs from the Seventh SS Division who were summarily executed, after they surrendered at the end of the war. The Serbs committed a war crime when they did that. The Americans were showing me more pictures, seeing if I could identify any. I thought the Partisan soldiers were responsible, but the Americans said that there were execution squads that did most of the dirty work."

"That seems like a reach. Were you able to put your finger on anyone for them?"

"Just one more. I recognized him because he came from Belgrade to see Josip just a couple of days before he was killed. And I prepared dinner for them at the house. The talk that night was all about the 'Cominform Resolution'. I gave the Americans his name and told them everything that I knew about him and about what I overheard that night."

"Are they finished with you?"

"They said for me to rest a few days, and then they want to talk about my walk from home to Weilheim."

"Just relax Ludwig. We just want information and nothing that you say will be held against you. So, we understand that it was you and your buddy, 'Curley', who met Konrad and Stefan with the motorcycle they used to escape."

"Yes, that's right."

"The woman who set up the meeting, would you be able to identify her?"

"I don't think so. She kept a scarf over her face. My impression is that she was Romanian, from her dialect, but that's about it."

"Okay, that's not important. But we do want to talk to you about a little bit just before that. Your unit was activated and sent into Budapest to the Castle. Did you know right then, as you were going, that Regent Horthy was being forced to resign?"

"No, none of the soldiers knew what was going on. I do remember noticing, while we were going through the middle of the city, that the civilians weren't friendly. I chalked that up to the tanks that were with us. Then when we got there, the Hungarians at the Castle weren't happy about us being on their doorstep. But it wasn't until late that afternoon, when they started shooting at us, that we realized it was serious. We were ordered to shoot back, but none of us wanted to kill Hungarians, so we all had bad aim."

"How did you, yourself, feel about Horthy's abdication and the take-over by the Arrow Cross?"

"Not good, but we all followed orders. The Russians were closing in on Budapest. That was our only concern at that time. And, we were soon back to our base and right after that ordered into the trenches."

"And the rest of your comrades in the 22nd SS, you think were of the same mind?"

"We all liked Horthy and most detested the Arrow Cross, but it wasn't something that we talked about much day-to-day. Like I say, we had a lot of other things on our minds."

"Now think back to December, 1944 when the 22nd SS became part of the IX SS Mountain Corps and Pfeffer-Wildenbruch is appointed its commander. What was the feelings about that in the ranks?"

"Everyone took that as a bad omen. We all knew that he was a policeman and not a soldier. The rumor circulated that the other generals were saying, that at best we were being led by a good politician. Even his command center was set up on Castle Hill, in the middle of the government area. When he got the Knight's Cross in January, and we were all trapped at the Castle and starving, now that was a real joke."

"At the end, in February, 1945, when the IX SS Mountain Corps was ordered to breakout from Budapest and reach the German lines, you were allowed to stay behind. Why was that?"

"I had been wounded around seven weeks before that day and hadn't yet been cleared for duty. Lucky for me since most of my comrades were killed."

"Do you know that Pfeffer-Wildenbruch, and most of his staff were able to surrender to the Soviets? He was wounded and taken prisoner, but he survived. He is scheduled to go on trial any day."

"I can only hope that he gets a nice long sentence. That's what he deserves. He allowed the Arrow Cross to have free reign and kill a lot of innocent civilians."

"Okay. Thank you for all this information. That should do it for you. But we need you to wait here at this facility, until we finish with the other three in your group."

"Stefan, you're quite the hero, I see from your file."

"Who do I have the pleasure of speaking with this evening?"

"You can call me Thomas."

"No last name?"

"Smith. Agent Thomas Smith, if you'd like to be formal."

"That won't be necessary. What would you like to talk about?"

"First let me thank you for your assistance to the CIA while you were in Weilheim. On both occasions you were very professional. But we will still need to ask you about two topics. The first is your service with the 7th SS Volunteer Prince Eugen Division.

There have been a number of war-crimes committed by that division in Serbia."

"None by my Company, while I was in command."

"That's true enough. But right after the battle, where you were wounded, there were a number of instances where they were involved."

"I maintained military discipline and would not allow such things. But I understand now that the commanders who replaced me did not punish violence against civilians, or even worse ordered it."

"How . . . What was the difference while you were there?"

"Training, discipline, order, morale. These were the responsibility of the Hauptleute, the Captain and his junior officers and sergeants. The division's senior offices set the strategy and expected the Hauptleute to accomplish them. My unit was made up of Swabians, Croatians, Magyars and others. In civilian life they would not get along. But in my unit, they were soldiers, brothers-in-arms and there was no divisiveness permitted. Anything like that was dealt with immediately. Then we were surprised that night at the Sutjeska River, by a larger force. After being forced to retreat, we regrouped in the dark, and in hand-to-hand fighting recovered our positions and heavy weapons. Then, we really laced into them. I am still very proud of my men, for their bravery that night."

"Well after you were wounded and hospitalized they participated in civilian massacres. That's a fact."

"It's easy for a unit to go bad when they're in action against guerilla forces. Sure, we needed sometimes to carry out tough questioning, to get information. But there were never revenge killings of POWs or civilians while I was there. But, yes, I knew that it was being done by other units and that maybe my men participated in such things later on."

"The second thing that we need to talk about is your flirtation with the Arrow Cross, while you were in Weilheim. They apparently got you out of the hospital in Czechoslovakia before all the reprisals started. Your allegiance switched from Hungary to Germany right after that."

"Well, here's the way that went. I was still recovering from an infection at the military hospital in Bratislava. When the war ended, sentiment against all Germans, even Swabians, ran very high almost immediately. The orderlies knew that I had been awarded the Order of the German Cross in Gold. For a Swabian that was almost like winning your Medal of Honor. An orderly was in the Arrow Cross and arranged to get me out of there before I was summarily executed. They got me to Weilheim through Austria. Hungary threw me out with the rest of the Swabians. Germany accepted us even with all of its own problems. So, yes, I gave my loyalty fast to Germany, but not so fast to Arrow Cross. I was looking at them but didn't like what I was hearing. I have never hated Jews. What ended my flirtation with them was when I saw them setting up, after the wedding, to attack the villa. My family was there and I defended my people as best I could. Took out a machine-gun, then a sniper position and gave misleading information to those attacking the underground bunker. Now even better, I have a chance to be an American and couldn't be happier. This is a great thing for me."

"We will want you to give us the names and all the information that you remember about the Arrow Cross membership in Munich."

"Yes. I understand and will be happy to do that."

"If you will, go back to your room and write down a list of names and when you think that it is complete, we will meet again."

"Good morning Sophie. Thank you for coming early. We have two things to talk about today. Your walk from Apatin was a real accomplishment. Not many people could have done it. What I'm really interested in today is when Herr Butscher was killed. You said that you were approaching the Drava River when the two men attacked you. Do you remember, was that the first time you reached the river from the south?"

"Yes, as I remember, we reached the river just after the attack, and then the road takes you away from the river a little as you go along."

"Then that would mean that Herr Butscher is buried at Saint Niklas an der Drau."

"Yes, that sounds right. I think that's the name. It's so hard to remember."

"We've checked. There's no record of him there, but we'll try again. What I'm really interested in though is the two men. Would you say that they were locals, Austrians?"

"Yes, that's the way they sounded."

"And then what happened to them. After Herr Butsched hit the one with a rock and the other stabbed him."

"The first guy fell to the ground and lay there. The second got Mathias from behind. He was able to turn around and fend off another attempt to stab him. Then the stabber helped the other one up and they went off. They went in the opposite direction from the one that we were going. As soon as I was sure that they had gone, I tried to stop the bleeding."

"When the attack first started, why do you think that they were trying to rape you?"

"Because of the disgusting things they were saying, that's why."

"Now let's talk about the machine-guns."

"Machine-guns?"

"Yes, the MG-42s that you and Konrad were getting for your future husband, to send to the Partisans."

"Oh, those. What about them?"

"Where were they coming from?"

"That seems so long ago. Do you need to know about that now?"

"Yes, you never know what might be useful for us."

"They came out of Romania after Stalingrad. Some Romanian by the name of Draza had a whole bunch of them stored across the river in Croatia. Konrad started doing a crate at a time. Then I threw my money in with him and we were able to do more. Draza was Josip's contact, but we were acting as the middle-man and handling the money exchange and conversions."

"Yes, we are very interested in how the money was converted."

"Oh, that. Well. . . ."

Just tell me. I'm only looking for information and not trying to punish anyone."

It's a little delicate. The local bank manager was a client of mine from my other business.

"You had another business? What were you selling?"

"Can I just say pleasure and leave it at that?"

"Yes, I understand now. We didn't know that. Do you think that Draza is still there and has one or more routes open?"

"I have no way of knowing, after all this time and all that's happened. But he was pretty resourceful. My impression was that his routes were very long standing. If he's not there, the routes are more than likely in full use. Money talks as they say."

* * *

"Good afternoon Konrad. Thanks for joining me today."

"Sure, my pleasure."

"We've gotten a lot of good information from your family members and they'll be free to go on their way, once your issues have been resolved."

"I thought that everything was good and that you just wanted to debrief us."

"That was the case until the British learned that you were here. Your currency manipulations for the East Germans are a big issue for them. Lloyds of London has lost some money, because of you. They want to recover as much as they can. Their representative wants to join us today. His name is Colonel John."

"I don't think that I'd like that. Everything that I did was for the East Germans or the Russians. He should talk to them. This wasn't our deal. They have everything."

"Well not quite everything."

"He's not looking to take my Inn at Lake Placid, is he? That's our only source of livelihood."

"You'll have to work that out with him."

"Please come in and join us, Colonel John, this is Konrad Butscher."

"Good to make your acquaintance Konrad. Please call me John. Did you know that a good friend of mine is part of your extended family?"

"Who would that be?"

"Your nephew, Adam's, wife's aunt, Countess Ilona Edelsheim Gyulai. I met her in London, where she was raising funds to support her father-in-law, Admiral Miklos Horthy. Small world, wouldn't you say?"

"I didn't get to know her well, while I was in Weilheim these past months. She was traveling all the time to London, as you say, and here to America."

"Yes, she's quite busy. Anyway, let's talk about your predicament. Lloyds has lost a tidy sum in their insurance, reinsurance and bonding markets. Your currency manipulations covered a wide spectrum of their business and your name is legend, so to speak, with the syndicates' Underwriters."

"Always, I was acting for the East German and Russian governments; under duress, I might add. In the end, I had to escape across Checkpoint Charlie, at the risk of my life. My usefulness to them was rapidly coming to a close and it was only a matter of time for me. The Germans and Russians are the ones who profited. Not me."

"Well there is the matter of your Inn."

"My family lost their Inn in Apatin, and now we have the one in Lake Placid. A fair exchange in my mind."

"The Underwriters are aware of all that you've said, but still they are left holding the stick, while you are even in these matters."

"What are they proposing?"

"They don't wish to be innkeepers. You are the one in that business. Their business is finance. They wish to hold a mortgage on your property. Say a twenty-five-year note. In exchange they will use their influence on the Olympic Committee to have the Winter Olympics there again. You will make a lot of money during the Games. It will be at some point in the future. You understand that the scheduling of the Games to different countries is very political. So, it may take some years to fulfill this commitment to you. But they will make this promise as gentleman to gentleman. Meaning that it won't be in writing."

LAKE PLACID

In 1950, kosher food was not available at any of the Adirondack Mountain's resorts or restaurants. Jews, were, as a result, discouraged from visiting the Adirondacks. Everyone agreed that, they should instead, continue vacating in the Catskill Mountains.

Human-nature remained unchanged with respect to the "other".

Konrad and Magdalena and their children, Mathias (seven years) and Anna Elizabeth (eighteen months), were living at the Inn; as were Great-Aunt Sophia Stambolic and Uncle Ludwig Genser. The adults all worked there. Its Grand Reopening was set for the Memorial Day weekend. The family was making every effort to fit in with the customs of their new community.

Paul and Anna Theer resided at their home in northern Virginia, across the Potomac from Washington. Their three-year-old daughter, Elizabeth, was helping Mommy get the house ready for her new brother or sister. Paul's career had advanced to the point where he was no longer being posted to foreign assignments.

Stefan worked as a security contractor, for various firms in the Buffalo/Albany area. He had "secret" clearance with the CIA. As part of his work, he traveled extensively around the world. Clients included manufacturers of: cameras and film; large electric-generators; locomotives and railcars; leather goods; and drugs. He continued field-testing weapons for the military.

Miklos Horthy Jr., with the help of Portuguese diplomats in Switzerland, arranged for he and his parents to move to the seaside town of Estoril, Portugal. It was surrounded by a wall built by the Romans. They would be safer there.

Admiral Horthy was writing his memoirs, "Ein Leben fur Ungarn" in English "A Life for Hungary". He never lost his hatred for communism and blamed Hungary's alliance with Germany on fear of the "Asiatic barbarians" of the Soviet Union.

Countess Ilona Edelsheim Gyulai arranged her family's financing, through sources in London, New York, Washington DC, Zurich and Rome. In London, she met Colonel John Wallace Guy Bowden of the Queen's Own Hussars, whom she would eventually marry.

Adam and Zsofy Diplich moved to New York City, after the rest of Zsofy's family moved to Portugal. With the help of the CIA, both of their green-cards were issued without a waiting period. They applied for citizenship shortly thereafter.

Theresia Diplich remained in Weilheim praying for her son, Mathias, to return alive from somewhere in Russia.

Nicolette Horthy moved to Tuscany, trying to get over her disappointments and indiscretions.

The Adirondack Mountains are in northeastern New York State. They form a circular dome, about 160 miles in diameter. Lake Placid is roughly in the center of its northeast quadrant, far from any large town.

These mountains are heavily forested. After the Revolutionary War, the people of New York State needed money to discharge war debts. The state government sold nearly all the original public land for pennies an acre. Lumbermen were welcomed with few restraints, which resulted in massive deforestation.

In the early Twentieth-Century, the Adirondack Park was created by New York State. In 1912, New York clarified that the Park included the privately-owned lands, of over a hundred towns and villages, and numerous farms and businesses. Inclusion of human communities made it one of the great experiments in conservation in the industrialized world.

About half the land was privately owned, but heavily regulated by the Adirondack Park Agency. Over the years, these regulations have withstood challenges from many interests including lumbermen, hydro-power projects and large-scale tourism development.

Memorial Day, 1950 was clear and cool in the Adirondacks. The three-story Inn's white plank walls sparkled in their reflection from Lake Placid. The family's smiles were broad, as they checked-in their first guests. It was truly a memorable day for them.

"How is your first day going Konrad?" It was Hillebrand Mansfield, President of the Friends of the Adirondacks and prominent businessman and politician. Konrad had been briefed on him.

He had also been briefed on the "Association", as everyone called it. Founded in 1903, FOTA is listed as a non-profit, advocating for "the long-term protection and health of the natural and human communities of the Adirondack Park." It is listed as a conservation organization, but the locals all knew that in practice it is much more. It could make or break you financially and socially.

"You sure do have the old girl looking fresh! I want to thank you and your family for bringing her back to her former glory. And we see that you are using the name 'Lake Haus'. That's a good choice."

"Why, thank you. We could see the potential for her right from the beginning. What do they say? Location, location, location. As for the name, we looked at different combinations of 'Alpine', 'Lake', 'Swiss' and 'Swabian', to go with either 'Haus' or 'Chalet'. 'Lake Haus' was the one we settled on. Glad you like it."

"When did you see her for the first time, and decide to make the commitment to buy? I must have been out of town when you visited."

"Actually, it was sight unseen. My family took this one in trade for the one that we owned back in Europe. We wished to come to America and make our lives here."

"That must have been such a big decision, and such a big risk. Please tell me the story sometime. I know that you are too busy to chat now, but there is one thing that I'd like to pass along."

"What's that?"

"An invitation for you to join the Friends of the Adirondacks. It would be my honor to submit your name for membership. This is really a big honor and big opportunity for you. You'll meet and get to know a lot of important people here in the Adirondacks."

"Yes, I'd be honored to become a member. How nice of you to ask me. I'm excited to accept."

"I'll be in touch then. Good-bye for now."

When the big day was over and Konrad had a chance to talk with Maggie, he told her about the conversation with Mansfield.

"That's great! It will go a long way to how we all succeed in our new community. Even for Matty. He'll be in second grade this year at Saint Agnes. I've heard that being a member of the Friends works wonders with how the other students and their parents will treat him."

"How are his English lessons going?"

"He's very fast at catching on. Because he's young, I guess. But anyway, it's you and I who need to keep practicing, and using it at home for all of our conversations. Not like you do sometimes, when we are alone, and you fall back into Hungarian because it's easier."

"I know. I know. I promise that I won't even say that I love you, except in English."

"Well if you slip there, maybe for that I'll forgive you."

"I think that we won't be able to go to Mass this Sunday with all this business. This is crazy the way it's going, but good. Lots of guests staying and the restaurant was going all day. Now, if it keeps up like this all summer we'll be set."

In less than a week, Mansfield, called the Inn and asked to speak to Konrad.

"Hello Konrad, it's Hillebrand. The Friends' next meeting is a week from today on the 10th. My wife, Bunny, and I were hoping that you and Magdalena could be our guests there. We'll get you sworn-in."

"That's very nice of you, Hillebrand. Of course, we can. We'd be happy to join you." But Konrad was only thinking about how inconvenient it would be for them to be away from the business for days.

"We come right by you, from our home in Saranac Lake, when we drive down for the quarterly meeting. We can pick you up on Friday morning next week. It's about a three-hour drive to Niska-yuna. Don't worry the Friends has guestrooms right there. The dress for the social on Friday night is jacket and tie. The ladies wear party dresses. Then the meetings will be on Saturday morning, through lunch, into early afternoon. The ladies have their own luncheon, which is very nice. We'll get you back in time for you to have dinner at home on Saturday."

"Sounds like you've done this trip before. Where's Niska-yuna?"

"Right near Schenectady."

"Konrad! You should have asked me first. What were you thinking? This is a social disaster!"

"What's wrong Maggie?"

"My clothes, my hair and my hands. That's all. I can't go and meet important women, for the first time, looking like this! What am I going to do?"

"Oh, I didn't think of that."

"Konrad, Konrad. Let me call my sister Anna for help. This is really a pickle for me."

Maggie made the call to Anna; who after confirming all of her sister's sizes, then told Paul in no uncertain terms that Maggie was in desperate need of help; who contacted one of his most trusted people in New York with the sizes; who contacted Zsofy and told her to meet him the next morning at Bonwit Teller on Fifth Avenue; and Zsofy told her aunt, Countess Ilona, who was in New York City on business; which resulted in a day-long shopping spree along that famous thoroughfare; and then on Wednesday, resulted in Franc from Ladies' Clothing, Marie, the Countess' very own hair-stylist and Norma a manicurist coming highly recommended by Larry Fay's associates in Hell's Kitchen; to be in the back of a beefed-up maroon V-12 Lincoln Zephyr driven by Carl, no last name, a sort-of-ex-bootlegger; which was headed north on Route 9.

"These are wonderful! Maggie was trying on clothes and picking three, or maybe even four, outfits for the trip. Franc doted on her as she went back and forth to the bedroom she was using to change. When she finished choosing, it was Marie and Norma's turn to work their magic.

The result was, that on Friday morning when Bunny came into the lobby to get "Mr. and Mrs. Butscher", she and then later all the other ladies were highly impressed and even jealous. Maggie was not at all what they had expected. Round one went to her.

"I'd like to introduce Mr. Konrad Butscher and to put his name into nomination for membership in the Friends of the Adirondacks." There was a polite round of applause and a perfunctory vote was taken. No one voted against Hillebrand's new member.

"The most important thing for you to remember, being new to the Adirondack community, is that we care for these mountains. Most of our families go back generations in them. We protect them, and our way of life, fiercely. If you have any new ideas, just check them out with some of us before you try to implement them. We are good people but don't like anyone trying to overturn the apple-cart." said Harry Mitchell, Third-Year Trustee of the Friends, as he and Konrad were sipping Scotch on the patio after dinner.

"I can understand why. It's beautiful here." And Konrad understood all too well what he was being told.

The people from Manhattan stayed overnight at the "Lake Haus". Norma was up early walking along the lakeshore before heading back to the Inn. The plan was to get an eight o'clock start, so she just had time for a light breakfast. And then it struck her: *"One day, this would be a beautiful spot for my wedding and even honeymoon."*

She stood on the deck outside of the restaurant and pictured herself in a white gown, with Carl, their driver, standing with her. *"Oh no, get that thought out of your head. No way! And you've only just met him. All he did was wink at you that one time and now you're marrying him. My God, girl!"*

The drive back to Manhattan was uneventful. Carl dropped Franc and Marie outside of Bonwit Teller, before taking 42nd Street over toward the Westside.

"Where can I take you Norma?"

"Anywhere that you want." It just slipped out before she caught herself.

"How about a drink or two up at Jimmy Ryan's on 52nd Street, before we decide where to go for dinner?"

"Sounds wonderful."

And that was the start of their romance. Eight months later he asked for her hand.

"Before I decide I have a few questions."

"Go ahead."

"What will my last name be?"

"Smith."

"Any problem if we're married by a rabbi?"

"No, no problem for me, if it's okay by him."

"I'd like to have the ceremony at the Lake Haus up in the Adirondacks, where we drove to, the first time we met."

"That sounds nice. I like it there."

"Do you want to honeymoon there?"

"I can't wait. Anything else?"

"Nope. You'll do. I say 'yes', and that I love you."

Norma called and made reservations with Maggie for the Saturday on first weekend after Memorial Day. And then, a ten day stay for she and Carl, for their honeymoon. While a number of couples had honeymooned there, this would be the first wedding ceremony at the Lake Haus.

"Maybe this will start a trend." Maggie and Konrad told each other. It was to be a small party, between fifteen to twenty depending on how many of the groom's family attended.

They purchased inexpensive plates, cups, glasses, cutlery, carving knives, cooking utensils, cutting mats and a new cutting board, which they left unopened in their original packaging. They stored these for use on the big day. The rabbi would advise them, when he arrived.

They knew enough to know that meat and dairy had to be kept separate and not served at the same meal. Pareve foods like eggs, fish, fruits, vegetables and oils were neutral and could be served with either. But here their knowledge reached its limit. But they were willing to learn and wanted to make their guests comfortable.

It turned out that there were sixteen in the party: bride, maid-of-honor and her husband, groom, best-man, rabbi and his wife, bride's parents, bride's older sister and her husband and two teenage sons, bride's younger brother, and a friend of the groom and his girlfriend.

The June day was comfortably warm, with just a gentle breeze. The welcome dinner, mid-morning ceremony and luncheon reception had gone perfectly. Everyone felt that it had been a beautiful event and would recommend Lake Haus to their relatives and friends.

But a few of the Inn's other guests did not agree. Two suites were vacated early and other guests made comments that were overheard and reported by the staff. "Jew lovers", "Kike Haus, not Lake Haus" and "Filthy Jews, even in this beautiful place", were specifically mentioned.

That Monday morning, all of the wedding guests had departed, except of course the bride and groom. The telephone, in the office rang, and Konrad answered.

"Is this Konrad?" Konrad recognized Hillebrand's voice, but it sounded hoarse.

"Yes, it is. Good morning. Hillebrand?"

"What were you thinking!? You've made a big mistake and .... and . . . and I don't know how to tell you exactly, or how to help you recover from it."

"What do you mean recover? From what?"

"Did you have a group of Jewish guests and a Jewish wedding over this past weekend? Did you?"

"Yes, I did. My inn is open to all people. It was a beautiful ceremony and all the guests were very nice. Those who don't like it, and I did have a few guests who didn't, that's too bad. It's their problem, not mine."

"Well, it is your problem and mine too. The Friends' officers are not as open-minded, as you apparently are. You were, as politely as possible, told not to bring new ideas in here, without checking with the officers first. You've kicked over a hornets' nest. It affects me too, since I was the one who nominated you for membership. I really thought that you understood what you were being told. They want to see us in Niskayuna tomorrow."

"What am I, a school child called to the principal's office? I'm not going. They can kiss my ass!"

"That's another really big mistake. Don't you realize how tough they can make things for you? Failing inspections; not getting permits; deliveries not showing up as scheduled; payments for utilities being lost in the mail; services being cut off without notice; and I've only scratched the surface. Please come with me; make an apology; say that it won't happen again, now that you know; let me talk to them in your favor. That would be the smart thing to do. Please!"

"I need to talk to my wife about all this. Your warning is understood and appreciated. But this is a matter of principle for me. I've seen first-hand in Europe, what happens if a man just stands-by, when his community treats people like this. I have your number and I'll call you back in an hour or so."

Konrad went to find Maggie. "Please come with me to the office. We need to talk." And Konrad gave her a blow-by-blow on his conversation with Hillebrand.

"Do you think that I should go? Hillebrand was only trying to help, but it just doesn't sit right with me. Not to accommodate a Jewish guest because some people have their heads up their ass. I remember what my father wrote to us just before he was killed. The price of being a 'bystander' and not speaking out against wrong things, that go on in front of your nose."

"I know that you are good man, Konrad. I know that you are brave enough to stand up, for what we both know is the right thing. But, think of the problems that Matty and then Annie will face in school. People will treat them bad the whole time that they're growing up. That wouldn't be fair to them. While they are children, they won't understand any of it. I'm their mother, and have to ask you not to do this. We might even have to move out of here and give up our dreams. And you know that your stand will be futile. It won't change anything. People will still hate."

"I have to say that you are right about people still hating.

And that my actions, could just result in hurt for you and the children."

So, Konrad went with Hillebrand and swallowed his pride. The Friends' officers forgave, with the understanding that it wouldn't happen again. And it didn't.

16

ENDINGS

Mathias Diplich was released in 1953, with all the other captured soldiers of the 22nd SS Cavalry Division.

"Attention! Attention! All soldiers of the 22nd SS Cavalry Division assemble in front of their barracks!" The announcement came over the camp PA system. It was repeated at one-minute intervals for the next five minutes. For me that wasn't necessary, I went there immediately. Whatever it was, it was out of the ordinary, and I didn't want to miss it.

"Line up. Load into the trucks. Don't go back to your barracks for personal possessions." The Studebakers were back. I thought, "The same ones? It looks like." We were brought to the train station and given seats in passenger cars. Old and nothing fancy even when they were new, is the way I'd describe the cars. But seats none-the-less.

When we pulled into the Berlin station, we thought that we were headed home. But the announcement came, "Get out! You can leave us now. Get out! You can walk across the bridge and though the American checkpoint. Hungary does not want you. We don't want you. You are going to West Germany."

I thought, "Are you kidding me? After all my sacrifices for Hungary, now they don't want me. Why? Because my great-great-grandparents were German? That makes no sense. I was born a Hungarian. Grew up there. Went to school there. Fought there and saw my friend die there. I went through all of that for my country, Hungary! The whole world is crazy. Germany divided and Americans in Berlin! Everything has changed. What the hell is going on? Why can't we all just go home?"

"And my family? Who's alive? How will I find them if they are alive?"

At twenty-seven, he was hardened from the war and eight-year imprisonment. He walked across the bridge not knowing what to expect, but with his head held high.

"I'm just a soldier, but I've survived. *No one can say that I haven't done my duty. That I don't belong somewhere. That I don't even exist. Because here I am. God damn it, here I am!"*

He stood in line at the reception tent. When it came his turn, he stepped inside.

"Full name and rank in the 22nd SS?"

"Mathias Diplich, Corporal in the Panzer Reconnaissance Battalion."

"Let me see. Hum, you're listed as 'Missing', not 'Prisoner of War'. Do you have any identification papers or tags showing your name?"

"No. It's been eight years. Does it make any difference? I'm coming out of a POW work-camp, you know."

"You could be trying to assume someone else's name."

"Sure, and why would I be picking his name and not an officer's or someone like that? Ask some of the other men in line. We've all been in hell together. They'll tell you who I am."

"Not necessary! Here is your approval to apply for permanent residency in West Germany. Wear this name tag while you're here at this facility. See the Red Cross people in the next tent for help in getting settled. Good day. Next!"

He went on to the next tent.

"Good afternoon. Corporal Diplich, I see. Sit here at the table. I'm sure that you would like to find your family. Yes? Let's see what I can find. Do you have any clue as to where they might be living?"

"No."

After looking through her ledgers, "Looks like a number

of your relatives were living in Weilheim, but they've left for America."

"Which ones? I don't even know who's still alive. Give me some names."

"We have German residents emigrating to the United States: Konrad and Magdalena Butscher and their children Mathias and Anna; Stefan Butscher; Anna Theer; Sophia Stambolic; Ludwig Genser; and Adam Diplich and his wife Zsofy."

"Thank God! Adam is alive. He's my brother. He's married now. Good for him! There are uncles, aunts and cousins and even a great-aunt I think. She must have married and so she has a different last name. Good for all of them. They're safe over there. Now, how about anyone left in Germany, or even Hungary, if you would know that?"

"I wouldn't know about Hungary, but there is a record of someone who could still be alive in the Munich area. She was living at your family's Weilheim address until all the others moved to America. Then, there's no further record of her."

"What was her name?"

"Theresia Diplich."

"That's my mother. I want to go and find her."

"We can clear you for travel to Munich and refer you to our refugee office there. They will help you to apply for permanent residency in West Germany."

"Thank you. That's what I want then."

Mathias traveled to Munich and soon obtained his residency papers. He wrote to his brother in New York to say that he was alive. Then he began searching for his mother.

He found her Death Certificate on file in Munich.

"Name—Theresia Butscher Dipliich; Date of Birth—January 5th, 1909; Place of Birth—Apatin, Serbia; Date of Death—February 19th, 1952; Cause of Death—Tuberculosis; Nearest Relative—None known; Buried at—Gate of Heaven Cemetery, Munich."

The next morning, he visited Gate of Heaven and spoke with

the nun running the office. He was directed to the monument for unmarked burials. He stood at the site with tears running down his face, silently praying. Father Johann approached and spoke words of condolence. Mathias connected with this kindly priest, who soon became his friend and confessor.

Mathias was not comfortable in the outside world. He had been in the army and then prison for much of his adult life. He craved the safety of a structured environment. When Father Johann got to know him better, he suggested that he consider becoming a Marist Brother.

The Marist Brothers are a religious community of men that strive to make a difference in the world by ministering to at-risk youths. They work in schools and parishes. Marist Brothers serve as educators, counselors, spiritual directors and social workers. They strive to influence and transform the lives and situations of the young through Christ.

Mathias Diplich found his life's calling on the streets of post-war Munich where at-risk young men were in abundance.

In 1954, Stefan's home was in Gloversville, New York. This town's water is considered the best in the world for leather tanning. The water was so perfect for this, that the country's glove and leather products manufacturing had been centered here. Even though the city's leather was still shipped worldwide, labor costs had caught up with the manufacturers, and their work was now being done overseas.

As a result, there were a number of vacant mill-buildings in the town's center. These buildings could be rented inexpensively. Stefan did that, to use for storage purposes. He installed a large modern walk-in freezer. It came in handy for some of his work.

He was called down to a meeting, with his handlers, in Mount Kisco. It was a beautiful day as he drove south. He preferred taking the Taconic State Parkway for its scenery. He thought, "I wonder what assignment I'll have this time."

"Stefan, we have something that's perfect for you. Do you remember Draza, the Croatian guy with the M42 machineguns? We want you to go to Croatia and meet with him. He expanded his business over the years and now has all kinds of weapons for sale.

The British asked us for a favor, but we need to do this without the Egyptians and Saudis finding out. There are clashes all along Israel's borders. Palestinian fedayeen attacks, that are often organized by the Egyptians. They are mostly coming from Gaza. Israel is launching reprisal attacks. The Brits want arms shipments sent out to Israel as soon as possible. There's a lot of small-scale fighting going on. But we think it will lead to something much bigger, maybe the Suez Canal."

"I thought that we were friends with Egypt and not with Israel. Have we forgotten that plot where Israel wanted to disrupt US–Egyptian relations, by planting bombs at American sites in Egypt? Even though it failed, and eleven of their agents were arrested and Defense Minister Lavon blamed, are we just ignoring that?"

"It's led to Ben-Gurion returning as prime minister and we're hoping for a much better relationship."

After flying into Vienna, Stefan met his driver at the airport. The next day, they were across the border into Yugoslavia and then south into its Croatia province. That evening they met Draza at his warehouse complex outside of Zagreb.

"You wish to purchase weapons from me? Don't you Americans have enough weapons? What are they for?"

"All you need to know is that we will be a good customer of yours and pay in US Dollars. You will deliver what we buy to the docks at Trieste. We only have until October 26th, when the American and British troops are out of there. But until then, you can still get anything we want across the border."

"Yes, I know that. What type of weapons?"

"Let's see what you have and I'll pick as we go along."

"My weapons are in this warehouse." Draza slid open the large door. And they went in.

"Here are machineguns. M42s from Germany. They come six to a crate with the spare barrel included. Very good condition."

"How many crates do you have?"

"Eighty-three, I think. Haven't done an inventory in a while."

"How much ammunition do you have for them?"

"In the underground bunker, I have about two-hundred thousand rounds for them, which is about four hundred each. It works out to twenty-four hundred per crate."

"We'll take them all, split into two shipments, two weeks apart."

"All? We haven't even talked money. And with the transport to Trieste, it will come to three-hundred thousand Dollars at least. I can give you a final figure tomorrow."

"Okay, you do that. Now, let's see your other inventory, like mortars, anti-tank rockets or land mines. Got them?"

"Yeah. I have lots of those."

In the end, Stefan spent the full one-million Dollars, that was in his allocation.

"What route will you be taking?"

"They will come on the southern route through Rijeka. It's a little longer at 265 kilometers, but almost all of it is in Croatia, where we have our best contacts. The very end, the last thirty kilometers is through Slovenia, but we get through there, real quick, less than an hour, before they realize it. As long as the border at Trieste is open to us, and we're not held up sitting in Slovenia."

"It will be open. That's where the allied troops come in, the British and American soldiers, even though they're under United Nations authority."

Stefan was back in Vienna the next day. He took the train to Frankfurt and caught the next US Air Force flight back home.

✴ ✴ ✴

In 1958 Abd al-Karim Qasim, an Army general had seized power in Iraq and eliminated the monarchy. He did not like the fact that the Iraq Petroleum Company (IPC) was producing oil for the benefit of Britain and other western countries and not the Iraqi people. Qasim and Britain struggled for control of the oil revenues. He would have nationalized the IPC but feared a western boycott, which would have deprived him of the revenue he needed to keep his military satisfied.

In 1961, when Kuwait gained independence from Britain, Qasim claimed sovereignty over it. He was forced to back down when Britain sent troops into Kuwait.

Qasim was assassinated in February 1963 when the Ba'ath Party took power. Then nine months later there was a successful coup against them. Abd as-Salam Muhammad Arif took power. In April 1966, he died in a helicopter crash and his brother General Abdul Rahman Arif succeeded him.

During the early Sixties, the British military attaché in Iraq was Colonel John Wallace Guy Bowden of the Queens Own Hussars. He was accompanied to Baghdad by his wife Countess Ilona Edelsheim Gyulai.

Stefan visited the Bowdens several times in Baghdad, and stayed at their home. His professional services were on loan to them from the CIA. Now Colonel Bowden was being recalled to London.

Stefan thought, *"Now that they're returning to England, and I've survived to the ripe old age of forty-five, it might be time for me to hang it up. Maybe I should join Konrad's family in Lake Placid. But first, I have to go on this helicopter with Abd Arif, and evaluate his home's security arrangements."*

Stefan died in the crash. His body was recovered and returned to his family in the United States. Konrad had him buried at the

Cemetery of the Gate of Heaven, in Hawthorne, New York, which is near Mt. Kisco. His grave overlooks the Taconic State Parkway and is near that of Babe Ruth.

His cousin Ludwig took his death extremely hard. He and Stefan had been very close, and Ludwig never got over his loss.

In July 1968, the Ba'ath Party retook control. Ahmad Hasan al-Bakr was president and chairman of the Revolutionary Command Council. The communists were leading an insurgency in southern Iraq. The Kurds were causing problems in the north. The secretary-general of the Ba'ath Party, Saddam Hussein was given responsibility to find a solution.

A political deal was reached, since military means had not succeeded. The economy boomed as agriculture and industry were given priority over the budget for the army.

The Bowdens returned to London. The Countess became a celebrity there, as a mystic espousing a philosophy combining Christian and Islamic precepts. In the 1980's they purchased a home in Portugal, where she wrote her memoirs, "Becsulet e's kotelesseg" or in English, "Honor and Duty".

"Konrad, there's been a misunderstanding between us for almost a year now."

"I think that I understand everything, Hillebrand."

"First thing, let's stop being so formal. Call me 'Bud', everyone else does. May I call you by a nickname or something, Konrad?"

"Konnie, would be fine."

"I made you 'eat crow' down in Niskayuna last year and we haven't spoken since. It was necessary and let me tell you why."

"'Eat crow', I'm not familiar with that saying. But I can guess what it means."

"Not as bad as some things, but let's not get sidetracked."

"Okay, say what you want to say. You must have been working on this for a while."

"Yes, I have. Because it's important, that you understand where I'm coming from. I'm your ally on this issue, with respect to Jewish people. But you can't change the world overnight. There are just a few other Friends' officers who feel the same way as you and I. If we push the majority too hard, we'll just be voted out in the next election. I want to eventually get you elected as an officer. That will start to change the balance. Even then, we'll need a few more. And the current officers run for different positions, when their terms expire each year. So, they are still around and get a vote for another year."

"It's not that I don't understand all that you're saying and trying to do. You are more of a politician than I'll ever be. But I've seen first-hand what happens when people do things your way. For me it's too important to tolerate even for a short time. Maybe there are other officers who would come over to our way of thinking, if we took the lead. I'd like to be elected and then lead that charge."

"Konnie, it just won't work. There's too much prejudice up here. I can't take the chance of nominating you. Not at this time. Maybe things will change one day."

The selection process for the 1980 Winter Olympics consisted of one bid, from Lake Placid, United States. It was selected at the 75th IOC Session in Vienna on October 13, 1974. The only other candidate city to bid for the Games was Vancouver, British Columbia, but they withdrew before the final vote. The 1980 Winter Olympics, known as the XIII Olympic Winter Games was scheduled for February, 1980, in Lake Placid.

"How are you feeling today, Maggie?"

"Not that great, I'm afraid. My stomach just isn't right. I know. Don't say it. I need to see the doctor. If it keeps up, I will. I promise."

"I wanted to give you the good news as soon as I heard it.

Lake Placid was just officially chosen for the Winter Olympics in 1980. The Brits promised that they'd get it for us, and they have! The loan will be paid off next April, and then five years later we'll be up to our necks in tourists. I'll be sixty-five then and after that we can retire. We have to plan for moving near the grandkids, like we've discussed."

"What would we do with Aunt Sophie and Uncle Ludwig? She's seventy-five now, eighty by then. I can't believe how old we're all getting. And Ludwig can't live by himself. He never got over Stefan's death. And that was over eight years go."

"We'll worry about it then. Who knows what the future brings?"

"What rules do you think that the Association will come up with for the Games?"

"We'll have to wait and see, but it might be a good time to break the barrier on access for Jews. The kids are out on their own now, and I haven't forgotten. But it just never seemed like the right time. It was easier to just go along."

In 1975: Aunt Sophie passed peacefully in her sleep; Ludwig found Stefan's Nagant M1895 revolver and committed suicide in the woods, where his body was found a week later by a hiker's dog; and Maggie was diagnosed with liver cancer. She died, not so peacefully, just after the New Year. The two women were buried at the family plot in Gate of Heaven. Ludwig could not be buried there due to the manner of his death. Konrad had him cremated and kept his ashes.

✳ ✳ ✳

Konrad stood on the deck looking out over the frozen Lake Placid. A woman came from behind and touched his arm.

"Hi. I bet that you don't remember me. My name is Norma Smith. I was married right where you're standing in June, 1951."

"Oh my God. Yes, I remember you so well. How have you been?"

"Well good and bad. You know how life is. My husband, Carl, passed two years ago. Finally drank himself to death. I'm over it now, but I wanted to come for the Olympics, and to see your Inn again for the good memories that it holds for me. We became aware of the problems that we were causing for you and checked out early. But that doesn't mean that we didn't have a lovely time."

"Thank you for saying that. I always regretted the way that your stay ended. My family has always prided ourselves in treating our guests well. And that just wasn't right how my other guests acted."

"Thank you. Is your wife around? I wanted to see her also. She's a very nice lady, so welcoming."

"No, unfortunately she has also passed. Four years now, as of last week."

"Oh, I'm so sorry to hear that. Would you like to sit with me and have a hot chocolate?" That just slipped out before she caught herself.

It was March, 1990, and Konrad decided it was time to take care of some unfinished family business. He was seventy-four, and if he didn't do it now, it would never get done.

"Norma, I'm going to fly to Europe."

"You know that I'm terrified of flying."

"I know, dear. But you don't have to come, unless you want to. It's my family's affairs that I should take care of, while I still can."

"What will you be doing?"

"I want to spread Ludwig's ashes at the Inn that we once owned in Apatin. That was his home. It's the only fitting place for him."

"Isn't it dangerous to travel there? There's so much turmoil in Yugoslavia right now."

"I'll fly into Vienna, then take a regional flight to Belgrade and drive from there. As long as I stay away from Kosovo, Slovenia and Croatia it will be fine. Apatin is in Vojvodina. That province is with Serbia under Slobodan Milosevic. And say what you will about him, he has control of the situation there."

"I guess you know what you're doing, but I'll still worry."

"I'll only be gone for a week."

Things went as planned. Konrad flew from JFK to Vienna and caught his connecting flight to Belgrade. He spent Friday night there. Renting a car on Saturday, he drove to Futog, and went to his farm. The house was gone and the fields long fallow. It made him sad, standing there and thinking about what might have been.

Sunday morning, he attended Mass at Sacred Heart Catholic Church, where he and Maggie had married.

After Mass he drove to Apatin and checked into the Inn. Dinner was enjoyable, as was the music afterwards in the tavern. The next morning, he had coffee and a sweet-roll on the patio, said a silent prayer for Josip and surreptitiously spread Ludwig's ashes on the ground near the house. Then he drove to Gakovo where his mother had died. The local priest agreed to come with him, and bless the ground there with holy water. He flew back to Vienna on Tuesday morning.

At the airport, he rented a car and drove to Saint Niklas an der Drau near Villach, Austria. His father was most likely buried there. He put flowers on the monument for the unknown, and had a priest there pray with him. He was back to Vienna on Wednesday, in time to check into a hotel at the airport, and have dinner. His flight home to JFK was early Thursday.

But, he gave into temptation and changed his ticketing at the airline counter. He would fly to Berlin before returning home. In November, 1989, after rioting by its citizens, the East German government had opened the Berlin Wall. People were free to travel throughout Germany. That government fell shortly afterwards and the country was reunited. The Wall was in the process of being demolished and Konrad wanted to witness that happening.

He spent the night at a small hotel in what had been the American Zone. In the late morning, Konrad walked and enjoyed the sight of the Wall slowly being torn apart. There were large official border-crossings and smaller unofficial gaps made by the residents of Berlin. The official start of the demolition wasn't for a few months. And then he strolled through Checkpoint Charlie and up toward the Leipziger Strasse where his office had been.

It was a warm Spring day and he suddenly became hot and tired. There was a shaved-ice vendor on the same corner, as he remembered. The confection was sold from a tricycle with an ice-chest at the front. An old woman was ringing its bicycle-bell. He stopped there. The street was much busier than he remembered. All the activity and noise was disorienting him.

"I'll take a lemon," he said, thinking, "She just looks so familiar."

The old woman said, "The leg seems to have healed nicely. Hasn't it, Konrad?"

"What!? No, it can't be you! You're dead!"

With her left hand, she reached across and lifted her skirt. With the right, she pulled a switch-blade from the top of her stocking and flipped it open.

All the while saying, "I knew you would come. You couldn't resist seeing the Wall come down. I took this crappy job and waited for you. My twin-sister would be alive, if it weren't for you and that damned air-raid siren."

And she threw the knife expertly at Konrad's chest.

AUTHOR'S NOTE

During my life, I've seen many changes in our society. America's acceptance of racial and orientation differences has certainly improved. But not so much for those of different beliefs, religious or political. Computers, social media, "the pill" and ICBMs have come into our lives, but human nature hasn't changed at all.

I read a book recently, and it got me thinking. It was about the duty of a bystander to intervene when a victim was being injured. The author's family had been victimized in the Holocaust. The main point of his book was, that by not acting, the bystander becomes complicit.

While the author had a good moral point, I found his proposed solution impractical. Mostly because it was inconsistent with human nature, being what it is. But regardless, he was right about there being a duty to do something, to act when we see evil.

When in my life, had I not acted against something I knew to be evil? When was I too busy with my marriage, my children and my career, with no time or little energy to act?

There are so many ways a victim can be injured:

- physically;
- financially, such as taking or denying things of value, like jobs, sales, or the ability to rent a property;
- emotionally; and
- socially.

It's important to understand how a person gets "victimized". It's human nature to divide into tribes. Whether by race, sex, orientation, wealth, age, politics, religion or language, we divide into our tribes and shun those we think of as the "other."

I read in a recent *National Geographic* about a former US State Department official, who is a founder of Genocide Watch, a non-profit that works to prevent mass murders. He has helped identify the stages that otherwise decent people go through before committing genocide.

It all starts with one set of people defining a target group as the "other." The next stage is claiming that this "other" is a threat.

Characterization of the "other" as sub-human follows. That erodes empathy for them. Society becomes polarized and its, "Either you're with us or against us." Geocide is not far behind, he posits.

Where does our society stand on this slippery slope? Consider our treatment of anyone who holds a different view than we hold. When someone in our tribe is denigrating their "other," what should we do? Just remain silent and avoid hostility? But if these attacks are unrelenting, how long before it gets out of hand?

Who is your tribe's "other"? Are you contributing to some-one's dehumanization? The erosion of empathy? What will you do?

And, what should I do at my age?

A wise man wrote, "God has created me for some definite service. He has committed some work to me which He has not committed to another. I have a mission. I may never know exactly what that mission is in this life. . ."

I've decided to write this book.

www.ingramcontent.com/pod-product-compliance
Lightning Source LLC
Chambersburg PA
CBHW030514130726
47901CB00013B/656